THE LAST GASP

AN EVER AFTER MYSTERY

CHAUTONA HAVIG

ISBN: 978-1-951839-26-0

Celebrate Lit Publishing

304 S. Jones Blvd #754

Las Vegas, NV, 89107

http://www.celebratelitpublishing.com/

To Meredith, who turned my dreams of writing about an illusionist's assistant into ashes--literal, "cigarillo girl" ashes. Thanks. This story is better because of it (possibly because Cinderella as an illusionist's assistant is just weird!). And thank you for being a delightful part of our Bible study but even more, for being my friend.

ONE

Gary Prinz stepped out of the California sunshine and into the role of Garrison Prince, rising Hollywood royalty.

An unfashionably buxom receptionist bustled toward him in miserable-looking tweed. "Oh, Mr. Prince. Everyone's waiting! So exciting. Come, come…" A second glance at him hinted she disapproved of his trousers, rolled-up shirtsleeves, and lightweight sweater vest. "You might have worn a sport coat at least."

Everyone's waiting? Sport coat? What for?

A few people waved as the woman trotted down the hallway, chattering about her excitement regarding the night's premiere. "I won't have tickets, of course, but I just know everyone will love *The Stolen Title*. It's sure to be your best work yet!"

"I hope so, Miss Fischer. I hope so."

The way she paused, as if for dramatic effect before flinging the door open, provided a hint of warning. Mr. Walker greeted him—Werner, if anyone did any digging, but German surnames were still out of fashion in America after the Kaiser and The Great War. "Come in, come in, Garrison.

Our prince has arrived… We even have Eva here to celebrate with you. No champagne, of course. Must comply with Volstead, but…"

Only because this room is full of press reporters? Why?

A sick feeling shook his belly. *If the picture is already a flop…*

One cheeky man with a thick Brooklyn accent asked, "How do you feel about your new contract, Mr. Prince? Are you eager to begin work on this new project of Walker's?"

The sick feeling turned cold. "I won't be doing that, gentlemen. I—"

"Oh, don't be modest, Gary." Walker turned to the men clustered around the edge of the large office. "Can't give away our studio's secrets, but I can assure you that Garrison Prince is at the forefront of sweeping changes here at Imperial Studios."

Uncertainty kept him silent. His gaze traveled about the office, taking in opulence he hadn't noticed much after being invited into Walker's inner sanctum in recent years. Like many men in Hollywood, he'd come from New Jersey, signed on as stunt and grunt man, and only out of sheer luck hit on a good contract when someone noticed that he had a handsome face that movie goers would like.

Eva, in long, languid movements, moved to his side and looped an arm through his. "Isn't this a scream?"

It should have been said with emphasis and enthusiasm, perhaps with a giggle at the end, but the woman's tone always sounded utterly bored. Gary shrugged. "I don't know—?"

"Your contract, silly. I've seen it—or my equivalent. It's the best my lawyer has seen."

"I'm happy for you," he began.

Walker preempted him. "Come, come. No time for chit-chat. We have a premiere to attend, but first…monumental business in the form of this six-year contract! The highest-paying one we've ever offered!"

Gasps and murmurs accompanied the fevered scribbling of pencils on notepads.

Lord, help me. Once I do this, I'll never work in this town again—even as a soda jerk!

Walker held out a fountain pen. "Garrison?" There may have been an implied question in there somewhere, but Gary only heard the iron-clubbed threat beneath it. *Sign it.*

He stepped back and out of Eva's grasp. "I apologize, sir." *A little deference wouldn't hurt.* "As generous as I'm certain it is…" He shot a look around him and prayed for the best. "And as flattered as I am, I distinctly recall telling you that I would not be continuing in film."

The men bolted from the room, each one pushing the other in their frantic attempts to be the first to a telephone. Someone swore. Another yelped. Somewhere, a door banged. Eva shot Gary a contemptuous look before turning back to Walker. "You'd better get me a good replacement, or our contract is void. Remember that. My lawyer will be in touch." At the door, she looked back at Gary once more. "You fool. You just signed your death warrant."

As if to make good on her words, the moment the door slammed shut, Walker began a tirade that began with how he'd caved to unreasonable demands for more money, which Gary had never made, and ended with something being flung at the door as Gary pulled it shut behind him.

The words, "I'll kill you for this!" rang in his ears as Garrison Prince stepped out of his role as Hollywood royalty and into the sunshine again as simply Gary Prinz.

A glance at his wristwatch assured him that there remained plenty of time to reach the park just a few blocks from Goldman's Taj Mahal Theater. And enjoy… another glance at that wristwatch… a couple of hours alone with Miss Lucinda Ashton. *Prinz soon, if she'll have me.*

Palm trees swayed overhead, and the purple flowers of the jacaranda trees sprinkled down on Lucinda Ashton as she strolled through the park to the bench where she met Gary Prinz most days. Her new dress hung just to the bottom of her calves, unfashionably long but not too much so. She'd set her hair in Marcel waves that she pinned neatly to the back of her head. Anyone with true fashion sense would notice she hadn't given herself a bob in the latest style, but it still blended her personal comfort with fashion.

Gary liked green, he'd said, and the colors of the dress, green with sprigs of golden brown and yellow, matched her eyes nearly perfectly. Lucinda's practical self said she should not be considering what Gary liked in her personal wardrobe, but honesty demanded she admit that she cared very much what he thought of her appearance.

He'd propose soon. Though he hadn't asked, he'd left enough hints to ensure that if she did not welcome his proposal, she had ample time to put him off. But she wouldn't. Gary Prinz couldn't have been more perfect for her if she'd sent the Lord God an order through a catalog store.

Pointed toed shoes that tied with neat tassels clicked neatly on the paving stones as she strolled along the path and seated herself on the familiar bench. Self-doubts began the moment she settled there. *I'm overdressed for a walk in the park. He'll think I'm too forward or something.* A dozen similar thoughts chased each other through her mind until Lucinda jumped up, ready to flee.

Gary approached, his face lighting up at her apparent eagerness to see him. "Cinda!" As he neared, he caught one of her hands in his and squeezed it. "Lovely dress. I don't know that one, do I?"

"I finally replaced my shabby blue one and decided to wear it."

A brief but definite examination of her in the dress produced a smile of admiration. "It looks made for you. I'm glad you wore it." He spread a handkerchief on the bench for her and grinned down at her when she sat. "I wish there were a photographer near. I'd love to capture this. Maybe someday I'll have time for a hobby."

"Maybe." Lucinda allowed him to take one of her hands in both of his as he seated himself beside her. "You look… excited."

"It happened. I received a reply to my application for admission to the Bible Institute of Los Angeles."

"You're in?"

Gary nodded. "You know what this means, don't you?"

Another of his hints. Was he trying to dissuade *her* or himself? She'd begun to wonder. "That everything you've been working for has become possible?"

When he nodded again, her heart began to race.

"I wondered, Lucinda…"

Now? Here?

"Would you consider having dinner with me tomorrow evening?"

"I have to be at the Taj by five o'clock."

For the first time since she'd known him, Gary showed impatience with the chokehold her job held on her evening activities. "Perhaps Sunday evening, then?"

"Of course."

The smile returned. "That's—that's swell, Cinda. Really. I have so much to tell you." He shot her a look. "To ask you, too." As if the ocean breezes kept passing clouds in front of the sun, his face darkened again "I've—I've kept things from you. I had my reasons, and I hope you'll understand…"

Kept things? What things? Why would he—? As quickly as the questions formed, Lucinda shoved them aside. Gary had never given her any reason to doubt him. She attempted a lofty, humorous approach. "Nothing illegal, I trust?"

"Of course, not. Nothing I'm ashamed of or should be ashamed of, even. However, I hope you will forgive me. I have given you every opportunity to see and know, but…" Gary shook his head. "Let's not talk about it now. You'll understand everything after tonight."

It all sounded complicated. While Lucinda had never been exceptionally clever, she was no ignoramus, either. Instead of showing her confusion, she asked about his day, and unlike his usual evasive responses, he pounced on it.

"I wanted to talk to you, but again, I can't tell you everything yet. You'll know tomorrow, of course. But…"

"Why? How will—?"

The way he took her hand and held it between both of his silenced her. Gary squeezed and sighed. Only then did she see how tired and… worried? Why did he look worried? She might have asked, but he stood and offered his arm. "Can we walk, Cinda?" Before she could answer, he changed his mind. "Actually, would you have time to take a drive? I want to show you something."

"As long as I'm home by four o'clock…"

"We'll get you something to eat, too. You think I don't know you often miss meals because you meet me, but I do. Let's go."

Slipping her arm in his always felt a little surreal. Gary was handsome—too handsome and intelligent for a simple cigarillo girl at the theater, even a nice one like Goldman's Taj Mahal. *And I'm not nearly pretty enough for someone like him.*

"That dress sure is nice, Cinda. I would have thought nothing looked better than your pinkish one, but this…" He rarely paid compliments of a superficial nature, but Gary stopped in the middle of the path and eyed her. "You sure are beautiful!"

"I am?" Lucinda tried to make sense of that compliment. "I mean, thank you but—"

"But?"

"Well, I've never imagined myself as anything but a pleasant ordinary." She flushed a little as she added in a slight undertone, "I mean, my skin is clear, and my teeth are straight. That's a blessing, but I'm not blind to the stunning women who parade in and out of the theater every night."

Gary pulled her arm through his again and moved just a little closer than he usually did. "Cinda, sometimes I think the emphasis on glamor in this town makes it difficult to see the true beauty that real people here possess." He gave her hand a significant squeeze and added, "People like you."

A cat came out of nowhere, streaking across the park as if something chased it, although nothing did. It shot up a tree, and as they passed under it, the little purple jacaranda blossoms showered down on them. He'd think her ridiculous, but Lucinda stepped away, closed her eyes, lifted her face, and felt the little flowers as they fell. "It's like a gentle rain," she whispered. "Only, you don't get wet."

"No..." Gary began.

She felt his hand in her hair, and her eyes popped open wide.

"But you do look like a starlet in an island film with an abundance of flowers in your hair."

The smile he gave her dimmed as she said, "Well that's something I'd *never* do. I've had more than enough of this movie mania from the Smith girls to last me an extra life or two."

"It's an honest profession," Gary argued. "Or rather, it can be. I know some people are ruthless, but—"

"But you haven't lived with an actress," she intervened. "I just cannot imagine choosing to live with one. If Mrs. Smith weren't one of the few women who ran an all-female boarding establishment that allowed residents to return after ten o'clock, I'd move."

They turned down the walk toward the corner of the park that led to her rooming house and the disliked Mrs. Smith. Gary slowed but didn't respond to her outburst as she'd expected him to. Instead, he said, "I've been thinking about Pasadena."

"Pasadena!"

"It's only twelve miles from the institute, and I did buy that Studebaker last month, so I can run back and forth to classes in just half an hour or so."

The only thing that kept her heart from sinking was the near certainty that he planned to propose. Otherwise, she'd never see him with all that driving time. However, he seemed to require an answer, so she said, "I've heard it's lovely there, but I've never been up that way." She gave him a sidelong glance. "I thought that's where some of the rich people had moved to get away from the city."

"Some have. There are impressive mansions, but they're building nice little bungalows, too—perfect for a family. It's quieter there—not so many movie stars crowding the place."

Too wonderful. I probably couldn't find a job there that would provide enough to pay for a rooming house… As if she'd tag along after him like that!

Gary led her to his car and opened the door for her. "Well, that's where we're going. I've found a house there that I think I want to purchase, but a man doesn't notice things like kitchens and room sizes in the same way a woman does. I'd like your opinion."

"Oh…" Her gaze met his over the top of the car door and she smiled. "If you think my opinion will be helpful…"

"I wouldn't buy the house without your complete approval. There are three I like, but one seems just about perfect."

And it was. After the half-hour drive to Pasadena, a thorough walk-through of all three houses, lunch, and the return drive to the park where they always met, they'd come to a decision. The smaller house on Oak Knoll Avenue would be perfect for Gary…and anyone who happened to live with him in the future.

As he helped her from the car, Gary made a show of looking at his wristwatch and sighed. "Tomorrow afternoon?"

"Of course!"

"And dinner on Sunday… even if things don't go well tonight?" That made no sense, but as she started to ask, he squeezed her hands, kissed her cheek—he'd *never* done that before!—and jumped back into the car before driving away.

Disappointment warred with delight as she walked back to the Smith's boarding house alone and still feeling the warm, firm, but soft pressure of Gary's lips on her cheek. *I've decided I do love him. Definitely. After nine months, one would assume I'd know my own mind, and I do.*

TWO

Screeches and wails greeted Lucinda as she tripped up the steps to Ada Smith's Boarding House (for respectable young ladies). That's how Lucinda always heard the name when Mrs. Smith mentioned it in conversation. All the residents knew that if Mrs. Smith could afford to stay without having to run the establishment, she would. However, she and her girls had arrived from some place in upstate New York three years ago, and when the money ran out, the boarding house began.

Some boarders, tired of the woman's uppity manners, whispered about there never having been a *mister* Smith, but that was only because the woman refused to speak of her husband. It didn't help that the girls sniffed when the subject of their father came up. He'd likely died in the war or from the Spanish Influenza or something equally tragic.

"If that Lucinda can get into the theater just selling her stupid gaspers and candy, why can't *we*? How are we *ever* to be introduced to the right people if we can't attend the same functions?" Ruby Smith's shrill voice would never make it on the stage, but the movies would like her pretty face.

Perhaps they prefer more than just a pretty face, though? It would be awful to have to work with her every day. Living with her for a few hours a day is painful enough!

Determined to make it upstairs without being heard, Lucinda crept into the sprawling Victorian house and pushed the heavy door shut with excessive care. She'd made it to the first step of the narrow staircase when a voice behind her sent familiar and unnecessary chills through her. "Miss Ashton."

Turning, and resisting the temptation to straighten her hat or dress, Lucinda pasted on a smile and said, "Good afternoon, Mrs. Smith."

"Please join me in the parlor for a moment, won't you?"

If you're evicting me, then Gary had better *be proposing on Sunday, or I'll be on the street in just a few short weeks.* When the woman gestured toward the wide pocket doors that were always left open except when the Smiths were in a private "conference," Lucinda nodded. "Of course."

A tray with coffee, a quartered sandwich, and a sliced apple had been set on the low table by the elegant sofa. "Please eat something, Miss Ashton. I know you often miss your supper, but of course, no one else is home when you leave for your position at the theater."

The unexpected bit of kindness unsettled Lucinda, but paying weekly for a meal she rarely was there to consume became expensive. "I appreciate the thoughtfulness, Mrs. Smith."

"It is what one does when one can. I would hope you would be as eager to help myself or my girls if we needed a kindness from you."

Oh, dear. What could she want? There wasn't anything to do but assure the woman that if it were in her power, she'd be all too happy to help with anything at any time. *I just hope it's true.*

"In time, we hope that the girls will be in a position to help you into better-paying employment. They must meet the right people first, of course."

"Of course."

Lucinda ate most of the semi-dry ham sandwich and half the apple slices while Mrs. Smith droned on and on about the auditions and parties Opal and Ruby had attended in the past month. "Of course," she added with affected sadness in her tone, "if the right people don't attend these things, how will they discover the girls' talents?"

"That would be difficult, I imagine. I wish I knew people to introduce them to. I'd be happy to do it, but…"

"That's what I was telling Opal the other day. I said, 'If Lucinda knew a director or producer, she'd tell us. Even a good actor or actress with some clout.'"

Inexplicably, Lucinda shivered. She fixated her eyes on the brocade-printed wallpaper and tried to brace herself for what might come next.

"Then Ruby had the most marvelous idea a moment ago."

The shiver repeated itself. "She did?"

"Yes. I'm surprised I hadn't thought of it before. You work at Goldman's Taj Mahal!"

That statement sounded a bit like saying a bird flew. "I do…"

"And all sorts of exciting premieres occur there. In fact," Mrs. Smith looked thoughtful, but Lucinda knew what she'd say before the woman added, "isn't there one tonight? With Garrison Prince and that Eva woman?"

"Labelle. Yes, *The Stolen Title.* They've spared no expense on this one, and there are so many secrets being whispered about."

Another long silence smothered the room. Lucinda watched the ornate Victorian clock with growing alarm. "Excuse me, Mrs. Smith, but I'll be late if I don't get changed. I did mean it, though. If I can ever help—"

"You could be at the back door at twenty minutes before the start of the picture to let the girls in. They'll wear their best frocks. No one will know they weren't invited, and perhaps they'll meet the right sort of people who can help them."

"I—" The idea wasn't just abhorrent to her. It was a recipe for disaster. "I'd lose my position if I got caught, Mrs. Smith, and then I wouldn't be able to pay my rent. It would be too great a risk, and it's really not right…"

When the woman didn't respond, Lucinda could only hope that Mrs. Smith was considering the reasonableness of her refusal. Nerves sent her fingers twitching, and to steady them, she reached for another piece of apple. Mrs. Smith rose and took the tray up with her. "I see. Well, of course, we cannot insist. I hoped you'd not only see the importance to us and benefit to you but also that you'd want to show some appreciation for all we've done for you. I can see I was wrong."

"Oh, no!" Lucinda jumped to her feet and pleaded for understanding. "Truly, if I can do anything that only inconveniences *myself*, I'd be pleased to. It's just that I do have to consider my employer's wishes as well as my landlady's. Can you see that?" At the slight nod she received, Lucinda repeated herself. "If there was some other—"

"I've misjudged you, of course." Though the woman's smile was small and thin, Lucinda had never seen it broader. She gazed at Lucinda for a moment and forced the smile open just a bit more. "Of course… I'm sorry. I do see it might put you in an awkward position. Perhaps you'd be so kind as to run down and get a small bucket of coal for the stove. I must get started on supper, and I've spent too long chatting with you to have time."

As if I have time to get changed into work clothes after our unnecessary "little chat." But despite the touch of snark that had entered her thoughts, Lucinda assured the woman she'd have it upstairs in a jiffy and dashed for the door to the cellar. Tremors ran through her and she froze.

"If it's too much for you, Miss Ashton—"

"No, of course not. It was just darker than I expected. I'll leave the door open for a little light."

"There's a chain hanging from a bulb. We had that put in when we moved in, and it has proven a wise investment."

With that to encourage her, Lucinda pushed the door wide open and began to clamber down the steps into the dank cellar. Halfway down, she froze as the room plunged into darkness. The distinct sound of the deadbolt being thrown into the latch told her it wasn't an accident. As if ripped from the scene of a movie she'd seen just the week before, Lucinda raced back to the top, pounding on the door and demanding to be let out.

No response came.

Do they only "hear" if you have subtitles flashing on the screens of their minds?

A SPIDER CRAWLED across the back of Lucinda's hand. Jumping and squealing, she brushed it off and banged again. "Someone let me out! *Please*! I'm terribly late, and this won't change my mind. I can't do it!"

No answer came. With each passing minute, the determination not to cave in became easier, mostly because with each passing minute, the chance of her not being let go became impossible. The manager liked her, but he couldn't allow unreliability.

Part of her said to give up. She'd lost her job already, and if Gary really did propose, she wouldn't need the horrible job anymore. No more selling candy and cigarettes to people who only poisoned the air of the nice theater with them.

The problem was that Lucinda didn't like the idea of marriage as a "rescue." She wanted to say yes without any hint of need behind it. *I want to say yes because I love him.*

Did she? That had been her question ever since the first

time he'd hinted he wanted to propose. She enjoyed being with him, liked their discussions, and loved how devoted he was to his faith. *Our* faith, she corrected herself. He'd explained that Jesus wasn't just a nice man who was tortured for being a rebel. He'd shared how even her evasion of truth was abhorrent to a truly holy God, and that torment had been designed *by* that God to keep her from eternal punishment. Such a beautiful and ugly picture.

She'd agreed that one would be foolish not to embrace a God like that. And so, she had. That made it *her* faith, too. Didn't it?

And I already decided this afternoon that I do *love him. I cannot allow this horrible moment to make me doubt it.*

A bang of the front door sent her banging again. Patty Anderson's voice came through. "Who's in there! What are you doing in our cellar?"

"It's me, Lucinda! Someone played a joke or something and slid the deadbolt! I am late for work!"

"Cinda?" The bolt scraped in the lock and a shaft of light came through. "Oh, Cinda! You look awful."

"Thanks ever so much." Lucinda pushed past. "I'm sorry to be rude, but I must fly and try to save my job!"

In a fraction of the time she usually took, Lucinda stripped her clothes off, tossed them on the bed, and began scrubbing to rid herself of the day's stench. Powder, a quick re-brush of her hair, and repinning the back to hint at the more fashionable bob waves. After that, she donned her uniform skirt and white shirt. Her bow tie eluded her. "Where did I put it? Where—?" A flash of red in her hand showed where she'd put it. "Oh, bother!"

Stockings clipped to her garter belt without ruining them, but when she reached for her work shoes, they weren't there. "Oh, I didn't take them out yet. Silly me!" Silly or not, they weren't under the end of her bed, either. Her house shoes weren't there, either. A peer under the bed showed her them there after all—one closer to the headboard and one on the other side of the bed. "Must have kicked—"

Lucinda reached as far as she could and felt around. One shoe… another. When she pulled them out, she found her old shoes, the ones she saved for if she had to have a heel repaired or something after breaking in the new pair she'd purchased just last week. With the clock ticking fast, she quit searching and pulled them on. Fingers trembling with the buckle, it took twice as long as usual to stand and survey the result in the mirror.

Her skirt hung lower than most girls' did—to the top of her knee. She'd asked for one three sizes too big and took in the waist to get it as long as possible. Some girls did the reverse, swearing the tips were better when you showed a little leg. *Tips might be better, but self-respect is priceless—especially when you make enough to put a little aside without them. Perhaps I'd have a different opinion if I were starving.*

Satisfied, Lucinda bolted for the stairs and took them at a half stumble. She'd raced out the door before Patty could tell her to settle down. Three blocks up, and Lucinda removed the jacket to keep herself from growing too hot, and half-trotted, half-jogged her way to the back door. "I thought I saw you come through already," Joe the door monitor said. "Just half an hour ago."

"Wasn't me. I'm late. Got locked in the cellar somehow."

The man shot her a look. "You all right? In there alone?"

"Aside from a spider who tried to get too friendly, yes. I put him in his place," she insisted, and it made old Joe laugh.

"Well, get on through. I'll be sure to let the boss know I saw you come in half an hour ago."

"Don't lie on my account, Joe!"

He patted her cheek. "But I did. I just told you I did. Not your fault I was wrong, but maybe it'll save your skin." As she dashed away, Lucinda thought she heard him add, "First

Theo's nosing about the place, and now Cinda's comin' in half an hour after herself. Strange night."

In the stockroom, a girl struggled with the tray, trying to swing it on, but everything slid right off. "Let me help—" She stared as the girl whirled to face her, red lips smirking at her. "Ruby!"

"I can't get these things on here with the tray in place, and I can't lift it all over my head without—"

"Well, that's because you're doing it wrong. But you have to get out of here, or they'll throw you out!"

"Nothin' doin'. As soon as the picture starts, I'm dumping it anyway. I just need to be able to get past that manager."

"I'll go tell—"

Another girl came in. "Newb?" she asked Lucinda.

"Um—"

"Yes!" Ruby stepped forward and held out her hand. "I'm Cinder's friend, Ruby. So glad to get this job. All the stars and—"

"Well, if Cinda hasn't told you yet, you'd better pretend not to notice they're stars. You'll get fired if Chuck sees you gawking. I don't even look at them. Sometimes, I don't even know who was here of a night."

Ruby pouted. "What's the point of carrying that heavy old thing if you can't enjoy the view?"

"It's called dollars, sugah. You're just a part of the furniture. Don't forget it." To Lucinda she added, "Better get hustlin'. I heard Chuck askin' where you are."

"Joe saw me come in."

A wink followed. "I'll let 'im know."

The moment the door shut behind her, Ruby shoved Lucinda against the wall. "Listen, you little mouse. You'll go out there, you'll do your job, and you won't say a word about me and Opal being here. Capisce?"

"Ca...what?"

"You're so old-fashioned! Do... you... un...der...stand?"

"I can't—"

Her hand closed around Lucinda's throat. Despite Lucinda fighting back, she couldn't wrest herself free. "I'll kill you *and* your precious fella if you don't keep your mouth shut."

How do you know about Gary?

How didn't matter. This wasn't her fault, and Ruby seemed determined to get herself caught without Lucinda's help. She nodded. *And I'll find a new boarding house tomorrow!*

Her lungs and throat burned as Ruby released her. She pulled a knitted bag from the corner of the room and skittered off with it. "I'll just hide somewhere until then. Keep mum, Cinder girl."

Your New York is coming out, Miss Smith.

THREE

Spotlights crisscrossed Hollywood Boulevard as Packards, Duesenbergs, and Rolls Royces turned out for the premiere of *The Stolen Title*. Reporters and fans lined the sidewalks in front of Goldman's Taj Mahal Theater, held back only by stanchions and red velvet ropes. From his seat next to Eva Labelle, Garrison Prince looked every bit the Hollywood royalty that Walter Walker wanted him to be. They'd pull up to the front door, step out, pose—all the things Garrison hated about his role in Hollywood.

"Walker is fuming, Prince. Don't be stupid. This isn't just a career killer. He has ties to the mob. If you cross him—"

"If he kills me, he still can't make me work, Eva."

She blew smoke through her nose and flicked cigarette ashes onto the floor. "A dead Prince is a boon to the film. Everyone will flock to see the last moving picture with the great Garrison Prince." She looked right at him. "I say it again. Watch your back."

If this talking picture thing works out like Walker thinks it will, you'll be a top star with that languid voice and your flair for vocal drama.

Reporters pressed in as he stepped from the car and

offered Eva a hand. The questions fired at him, one after the other.

"Why didn't you sign the contract, Mr. Prince?"

"Did Universal give you a better offer?"

"What will you do if you're not acting?"

Beside him, Eva stiffened. He couldn't blame her for being peeved, and Garrison had to do something about it. "Gentlemen, please. Tonight is about this picture. Eva has put hours of work into this, and my future career choices shouldn't detract from her shining moment."

Another car pulled up behind them—Walker's, most likely. Garrison led Eva up the carpet as quickly as was reasonable and did everything in his power to turn all the limelight on her. If the murmurs he heard as he passed meant anything, the reporters noticed and respected him for it. *Maybe that'll help.*

Inside, ushers led them to their seats—best seats in the house, of course. The Taj Mahal didn't just possess a facade of the onion-domed Indian palace, even the interior had gold plush, upholstered, mahogany seats, exotic patterned walls with pishtaq arches, great chandeliers, and silk draperies. Every time he sat in there, Garrison found something he'd never seen.

"Will Grauman's Chinese Theater be this grand, do you think?" he asked Eva over the music of the organist at the front left of the stage.

"Grauman is determined to outdo Goldman, and Goldman won't have anything to do with it," Eva insisted. "I heard he's pulling down the corner palms and putting up spires like on the real Taj. He's putting big spotlights in it to shine from all sides."

"It'll be spectacular," Garrison conceded. *But what a waste of money.* Conscience struck him. *Then again, people are making heaps of it these days. Without this industry, I wouldn't be able to buy that house, the car, take up studies at the institute* and *get married. I need to remember that.*

Just as the room began to fill, the cigarillo girls started up the aisles from the front. Lucinda came up his row as usual, and as usual, she offered her tray to each person without really looking at them. He'd been so surprised that first afternoon in the park when she'd asked the time, thanked him, and walked away. She really didn't know who he was, which meant he'd gotten to know the real her.

"Cigarettes? Candy?"

A nudge from Eva and a whispered, "Get me some gaspers, will you?" prompted his order.

"We'd like Goobers and a package of Chesterfields, please." The tip he left should have gotten him a bit of flirting. Most of the girls in the theater would have, but Lucinda's eyes were trained on a few seats behind him.

"Thank you, sir. Enjoy the picture, and congratulations."

"Thank you, Cinda."

Even the use of her name didn't get him anything more than an absentminded smile and no direct eye contact. While not unusual, she typically was more distant than distracted. *I wonder what has her attention…*

"Did you offend her?" After a sneering laugh, she added, "Flirting with the cigarillo dolls isn't quite your game, is it?" Eva added, "Butt me, would you?" before he could reply.

Gary would not miss the constant assault of cigarette smoke on his lungs after this final evening, but he extracted one from the package and lit it as she took a draw on it. He drew out the proceeding as long as possible because it allowed him to look back and see what had drawn Cinda's attention.

A girl back there—rather fast looking, as if hoping to be taken for a flapper but not willing to go quite that far—glared at him. *What have I done to offend you?*

When she shifted, so did her expression. She smiled and batted her eyelids as if she hadn't just sent death daggers at him seconds before. The house lights flickered, and he turned back to the screen. *My last picture.*

He'd prayed for months, knowing that contract was coming up. Thirty-five hundred dollars was more than the average American male made in a year, much less a week. He'd invested well in properties and gold as advised. That contract he'd refused—it had likely promised five thousand a week. Was he mad?

I'd be mad not to leave now and start a real life with Cinda—one that won't interest the readers of Photoplay.

The room plunged into darkness, and the flickering lights of the projector arrested the attention of every person in the room. Just as the organist segued into the opening song of the movie, Eva leaned over and said, "Did you hear? Walker has paid Feingold a fortune to turn Brontë's *Villette* into a screenplay? He's casting me as Lucy Snow. You could have been Emanuel."

"Instead, I'll be a student at the Bible institute," he whispered back and turned his attention to the screen.

"I'll kill you myself if this one flops because you abandoned me," she hissed back.

Garrison ignored her.

After two years of working at the Taj Mahal Theater, Lucinda could anticipate the shift of the music with minor notes the organist changed to ensure a perfectly timed wind-down. The lights would go on in thirty seconds. She grabbed two more packages of Chesterfield cigarettes, several of the new Charleston Chew bars, and packages of ritzier chocolates before rushing to the side door, ready to step out the moment the film paused for reel change-intermission time.

Repeated glances at the overhead light bulbs meant that when she stepped into the theater, she wouldn't have trouble adjusting her eyes. The curtains parted, and Joanna stepped out. Lucinda followed. The chattering of voices greeted them at the same moment the girls made their way to the aisle.

Bang!

Screams filled the theater. Lucinda dropped to the floor and scanned the room. *What happened? Part of the promotion? Someone pop a champagne cork? Is that what it sounds like? In here? With the acoustics?*

A piercing scream rose above the others. She heard a voice that sounded familiar shout, "Get a doctor! Eva's been shot!"

Men rushed the stage and toward the side exits to the back of the theater. Somewhere, a woman fainted, if the cries for smelling salts could be trusted. Someone else called out in a booming voice. "Please take your seats, ladies and gentlemen. The police have been called. No one is to leave."

Lucinda didn't recognize the speaker, but voices died down some, cries became quiet weeping and sniffles. Only a couple of hysterical women kept screeching. The sound of a slap reverberated through the room. One woman down. Another crack stopped the last of the hysteria as someone slapped the other woman.

Lucinda slipped off her tray and set it in front of the stage. She moved among the audience, offering comfort here, requesting someone lower his tone there. One man still stood trying to soothe a woman's hysterical sobbing. She hurried forward.

"Sir, I'm sorry, but they're requesting that everyone remain in their seats until the police arrive. "I—"

She froze as the man met her gaze and said, "Cinda, I can't. Helen is coated in blood from trying to help Eva."

"G-g-gary?"

"We'll talk later. Where can I take Helen? I can't make her sit next to her friend—not like this."

His words swirled in her mind until she managed to sort them into proper order. "Friend? Eva? Blood?" Lucinda's knees tried to buckle, but she ordered them to support her. A second glance showed it. Gary. A third look brought all the pieces together in one picture. “You’re Garrison Prince? Gary Prinz. I am a fool, aren’t I?”

“Not now, Cinda, please. I need to get Helen to where she can wash and be safe. Can you take her?” His familiar touch to her elbow snapped her out of the semi-trance that had taken over. “Please. We’ll talk later, I promise.”

Blood on the woman’s hands spurred Lucinda into action. “Come with me, miss. I’m sure they’ll allow us to go to the ladies’ washroom for just a moment. I’ll stay with you the whole time…” All the way up the aisle, one arm around the woman’s shoulders, Lucinda spoke soothingly and fought down the bile that rose at the sight of all that blood.

Not a champagne cork, Lucinda mused. *Gunshot. I should have known it.* When full realization spread through her belly, she added, *Please, Father. Help me not be sick.*

Eugene stood at the back doors, ready to prevent anyone from leaving. Lucinda stepped close and whispered, “She was sitting next to the victim—has blood all over her. Someone saw it all, so I think it’s safe to allow her to wash, don’t you? We can’t expect a customer to sit there covered in blood.”

“Mr. Easley said we were not to let anyone out.”

“I’ll be responsible, Eugene. I’ll bring her to the washroom and back myself. But Mr. Easley is not going to be happy if the studios complain about treatment of their employees.” The man looked doubtful, but scrawny Mr. Tubbs strode toward them, and Eugene hated the man.

“Go ahead, but be quick about it. I’ll hold off Tubbs.”

Only once they’d entered the small washroom did Lucinda realize that “Helen,” whoever she was, was still crying. “It’ll be all right, Miss… Helen. Let’s just get those hands washed.”

“So much… blood.” A shudder prompted a new fit of weeping. Her hands shook as she saw them for the first time in full electric light. “Ugh!”

"Let's just scrub those up nicely…"

Soap, towel, and a lot of water—it took all three and the patience of Job for Lucinda to manage to get the blood off Helen's hands, but where the young woman had tried to wipe them clean on her dress proved impossible. Instead, Lucinda pulled the dresser scarf off a low table, draped the beaded thing over one hip, and tied it to the other. "There. At least you won't have to look at it."

It wasn't the thing to question a guest about her actions, but Lucinda's curiosity overrode protocol. "How did you manage to get so much blood on you, Miss…"

"Just call me Helen." The girl's shrill voice only screeched more with emotion. "Papa called me 'hellion' when he was in a temper." Wide mascaraed eyes gazed up at her. "Why did I think of that at a time like this?"

"Shock, I would imagine."

"Oh." The girl—yes, that was a better word for her—blinked back further tears and stared at the streaks of mascara that disfigured her cosmetics. "Oh, blast! I look a mess!"

Already wetting a small towel, Lucinda wrung it out and passed it over. "We haven't any cold cream, I'm afraid. Sorry."

"You're awfully sweet."

That's when they saw that the girl's face wasn't just blotchy from crying. Blood had mingled with tears, powder, and mascara. "Oh, get it off me! Please, get it off!"

This time, no amount of soothing would calm Helen. Lucinda washed, rinsed, and washed again, repeating the process until Helen's face and hair bore no more traces of blood. Fortunately, the girl hadn't noticed a fine spray of it on her shoulders. "All right, Miss Helen. We must return so that no one thinks you're guilty of anything."

"Me! How could I be guilty? That madman could have shot *me*!"

Madman? As she led the weeping girl, who now looked no

more than fifteen, to the door, Lucinda asked, "Did you see who shot Miss Labelle?"

"Of course not! I heard the shot, screamed like every other person in her right mind, turned to ask Eva what it was, and saw all the blood coming from her throat. I tried to stop it." Eyes closed and shaking now, Helen said, "So much blood. She couldn't speak, and then…"

"We'll get you back inside and find you something to drink."

"Can you get me a gasper? I need one something fierce—to steady my nerves and all."

"I'll bring you some. I think Mr. Prince has some. He purchased some earlier."

"For Eva," the girl whimpered. "He doesn't smoke—says he can't imagine why anyone would want to. Religious nut. Did you know he quit? Mr. Walker is furious. Threatened to *kill* him." Eyes wide, Helen's age dropped by another couple of years in Lucinda's estimation. "You don't think *Mr. Walker* tried to shoot him and clipped Eva instead!"

More likely that he'd hire someone, but… She shuddered. *Gary… if the man missed…*

"Come on. We need to warn Gary!"

Helen stopped and scowled. "Look at you gettin' all familiar. Don't think Prince'll like that!"

What would you say if I told you that he was *probably going to propose on Sunday? That's probably over now.*

FOUR

Officers streamed into the theater just as Garrison finished cleaning off the tiny bits of blood spray from his face and as much as he could of the fine mist that had reached the front of his shirt. His tuxedo jacket he'd draped over Eva in an attempt at respect, although he'd read enough detective stories not to touch any more of her than he must. *Only the wrist to be sure she wasn't just unconscious*, he repeated to himself. He just couldn't think why he felt the need to do so.

Behind the officers, he saw Lucinda leading Helen back into the theater. Even from quite a distance, he saw that the freshly scrubbed girl was indeed as young as he'd always surmised. *Eighteen. Hardly. More like twelve if she's a day.*

When Lucinda looked back his way, she gave him a weak smile and returned to her ministrations. Garrison strode forward, but an officer stopped him. "You can't leave, sir. Please take your previous seat and we'll be excusing people—"

"I can't sit there. I was next to the victim. My seat has blood on it, and while I'm not squeamish, she was a friend."

Was that true? Did someone you worked with qualify as a friend if you hadn't planned on seeing that person again once you quit your job? Garrison didn't have time to elaborate before the officer said, "You still can't leave, sir." The man's eyes widened. "Sorry, Mr. Prince, but even you—"

"I was just going over to where one of the cigarillo girls is helping the other person who was seated by Eva."

The man blanched. "Not Eva... Labelle?"

"Fraid so."

"What's this world coming to when a fella can't even attend the moving pictures without having someone killed right next to him. Bet it's connected to the mob. I hear rumblings..."

Should you be talking to me about this?

As if he had the same thought, the officer said, "Go ahead, but I can't let you leave. You stay inside where we can talk to you. I know Detective Lindstrom is going to have questions for you and the girl." He leaned forward. "How old is that child?"

It took a moment to formulate an honest answer that would convey what he wanted to say. "Company records say eighteen."

"I see."

The back doors swung open, and a little man appeared. No more than five-foot five and as slight as a ballet dancer, only the suit, gray hair, and the air of authority that fairly radiated from him made anyone take note of his arrival. The officer stood at attention. "Detective Lindstrom—Carl Lindstrom," he whispered under his breath. "Don't look like much, but he's the best there is. Someone oughtta write detective stories about *him*."

Garrison inched toward Lucinda and Helen while the officer joined a couple of others, argued a bit, and moved to the back to guard the door with an aggrieved air. Several people tried to push past him, but the man held up his baton and waved them back. "In your seats, if you please. We'll move you out as soon as we can. A person died here. Show respect."

A few protests of, "Do you know who I am?" and "I'll have my lawyer on you!" followed that order, but the officer remained unmoved.

Garrison reached the girls and leaned close. "Are you all right, Helen?"

"I want to go home!"

"We can't." His heart clenched at the pitiful expression Helen shot him. "And they'll want to talk to you. We'll ask if Cinda can stay with you for that part, though." He gave Lucinda a pleading look. "You will, won't you?"

"Of course."

Helen, while not the quickest horse on the track, caught onto his tone. "You know her, Garrison?"

"Cinda's my…"

"We're… friends," Lucinda said with what sounded like excess firmness to Garrison.

No… why did this have to happen here? Now. Under these circumstances.

People nearby leaned close and asked, "What happened? Are you all right?"

Without mentioning the bit of blood he'd had to clean off, Garrison suggested that Helen had endured the worst shock. "We didn't know until we turned to say something to Eva."

"So, it's true," one man said. "Someone shot Eva Labelle?"

Helen began weeping. Cinda consoled her as Garrison confirmed.

"Why? Why would anyone want to kill Miss Labelle?"

That was an excellent question, one Garrison hadn't yet had time to ponder. Helen sat up, eyes wide, gaping at him. "Nobody! But everyone's mad as hornets at you!" Her hand covered her mouth but not enough to block her next words, "What if they tried to clip you!"

THAT ISN'T how I'd planned to warn him, Lucinda mused. *And why did you say it as if you'd just thought of it?* Even as she wondered, a cynical thought forced its way to the forefront of her mind. *You're acting. Even now—all for dramatic effect.*

The shock that Gary couldn't hide told her he hadn't thought of his being an intended victim. Voices around them slowly rose in a crescendo of disagreement. Some wanted him guarded while others wanted him removed from the vicinity before "he gets us all killed."

Rumors filled the air, but Lucinda only caught snatches of them. "—heard he's moving to Universal Pitchers."

Pictures, she corrected automatically. *Pronunciation is paramount.* A high-pitched giggle came from somewhere as she thought, *Or should I say,* Paramount*?* A moment later she realized the giggle was hers.

"Cinda?"

"I feel… giddy." This time, when her knees buckled, she forced herself to sit down—hard.

Gary reached for her and missed. He knelt beside her, holding her hand. "Are you all right? Should I ask for those smelling salts?"

"No… no. I think it all just hit me. The blood, the screams…" This time, she met his gaze and whispered, "You. Why didn't you tell me that you—?"

He leaned close and whispered, "Can we talk about it later? This was part of what I wanted to discuss on Sunday."

"You're moving studios?"

"He quit!" Helen screeched. "Turned down the biggest contract in studio history!"

"Why" struck her hard. *For the Institute. He wanted to go to the Bible Institute—to become a minister.* If the look he gave her meant what she'd always thought it did, he'd also done it to marry her outside the Hollywood life. *That's good… isn't it?*

What Gary said to that, Lucinda couldn't hear. An outcry rose in their section, and it spread, row by row, to the rest of the theater. He groaned. "It's not supposed to be discussed by studio employees until tomorrow. I'm still studio property until midnight."

"Like Cinderella!" Helen wailed. "Only you're Cinder's fella!" She giggled before hysterical sobs took over once more.

Oh dear, not only a terrible pun, but the hysterics! She started to rise, but Gary kept her seated with a gentle yet firm hand on her shoulder. "I'll get her help. You just rest."

Looking and finding were two very different things. Gary returned, supporting Helen all the way. He found a corner where he could block her from view and sent Lucinda a silent message. *Can you come?*

At least, that is what she thought the looks he sent her said. She rose, smoothed her skirt, tugged the cropped tuxedo jacket into place and squared her shoulders. Someone asked for a pack of cigarettes. Someone else requested chewing gum, "Wrigley's Spearmint, please."

Lucinda waved to Dotty, pointing out people requesting items as she went. At Gary's side, she whispered, "What happened?"

"That detective, Lindstrom, he said he's going to begin interviewing people right away—starting with Helen and me. He'll be calling us back in just a moment." In a lowered voice, he added, "I think they'll let you go with her—since you're an employee. Will you?"

She hadn't had a moment to consider when a thickset officer in a button-strained uniform stepped up. "Miss Fenwick?"

Helen's wide eyes looked even wider without the heavy makeup. "Yes?"

"Detective Lindstrom wishes to speak to you. If you'll just follow me."

Lucinda turned to him. "Officer, we were led to understand that the detective won't mind if I accompany her—as an employee of the Taj Mahal…" At the doubtful look on his face, she added in a whisper, "I very much doubt she's a day over fifteen, sir."

A glance at the girl beside Gary seemed to soften the man's features. "Of course, miss. Just follow me." He shot a penetrating look at Gary. "*You'll* stay here, sir."

"Of course."

Lucinda felt a slight squeeze of her elbow as she passed, and Gary's whisper, "I'm praying here, Cinda," added such a blissful moment of normalcy that she smiled before she could remember that she was angry with him.

Perhaps not angry. I shouldn't decide a matter before I hear it out, or whatever the proverb says.

They followed the officer through the side doors and down the hallway to the storeroom where a table had been set up. The man seated at the table looked like the homely brother of Rudolph Valentino, short, unassuming. *But his eyes would wrest a person's deepest secret from her before she knew what hit her.*

"Parker, I said I wanted to speak to Miss Helen…" He glanced at a sheet of paper beside him. "Fenwick."

Helen gaped, quaked, and began weeping again. Lucinda spoke up before the officer could get into trouble. "We were told that as an employee of the theater and since Miss Fenwick is rather…" She shot an apologetic look at the girl before continuing, "…*young*, I could be here to offer support. I'll keep quiet."

"Are you acquainted with Miss Fenwick—personally or professionally?"

"Outside of her occasionally being here at events, I've never seen or spoken to her before. I don't *recall* having served her before, but it is possible."

When Lucinda's hand trembled, she laced her fingers together behind her back and prayed it wouldn't travel up her arm. *Please don't ask me more questions. I'm at the end of my emotional tether as it is.*

"Very well. No speaking." The man's features softened when Lucinda couldn't avoid a wince. "I apologize, Miss…"

"Ashton. Lucinda Ashton."

He scribbled it down, glanced up at her, and scribbled something else. "As I said," he continued as he set down his pen and gazed at her. "I apologize. There was no call for me to bark at you like that."

"Of course, Detective Lindstrom."

The man's eyebrows rose, but he didn't respond. Turning to Helen, he began asking questions. Who she was, where she lived, when they'd arrived, and where she'd been when the shot rang out? That took her silent weeping into full-blown sobs. Lindstrom shot a look at Lucinda, but since he didn't speak, she kept silent. "Miss Fenwick, do you need a cup of coffee or…?"

The girl's face wrinkled in obvious dismay. "No!" Still the tears flowed.

Lucinda reached over and tucked a handkerchief in the girl's hand. "Here… it's clean."

"Th—thank you." A moment later, it was no longer clean. "She's ever so nice, detective."

"I see that." The smile he offered Lucinda softened features, but unlike storybooks, it didn't "transform his face" into anything but the same man who awaited a simple answer.

"I was sitting next to Eva—on her right."

She'd have corrected the girl, but a quick look from the detective silenced her. "Is that," he began, "her right or yours as you took your seat?"

"Um… well, Garrison was on the aisle seat, you see. Then Eva was sitting next to him. I was sitting next to her. Her right… isn't it?" The handkerchief took a full nasal assault before she added, "I've never been good with rights and lefts. Makes the director nerts!"

Nerts?

Her confusion must have been obvious, because Detective Lindstrom said, "And by that you mean he goes a little batty? Crazy?"

"And how!"

Lucinda offered an acknowledging smile to the detective. *That one I know.* She missed the next couple of questions as she pondered how even surrounded by current slang, she often didn't recognize it. *The phrases change so quickly! Perhaps one can be an old maid at twenty-four.*

"—did you do when you realized Miss Labelle had been shot?"

There Lucinda returned her attention to the conversation, and Helen shifted from upset young lady to… well, she didn't know what the girl was up to, but everything in her demeanor shifted. "Am I supposed to call her by her stage name or her real name?"

The detective picked up his pencil and held it poised, despite the fact that an officer in the corner had been writing down almost everything they said. "And what was her given name?"

"Edith Flint."

And you like being the one to announce that. Why?

As it turned out, she couldn't consider it for more than a moment. As soon as Helen had to try to describe stopping the blood, she lost her nerve again and resumed weeping. Lucinda gave the detective what she hoped was a look that offered to pick up from there.

"Do you have something to add, Miss Ashton?"

"That is when Mr. Prince asked if I would help Miss Fenwick to the washroom. One side of her was sprayed with blood—just a fine mist of it. Her hands were coated where she'd tried to staunch it before realizing that Miss Labelle was dead." Despite every effort to remain dispassionate and focused, she shuddered. "It took quite a while to get all the blood off her." She pointed to the scarf draped across Helen's hips. "That's from the washroom stand. It hid some of the blood so she wouldn't have to stare at it."

"She was wonderful!" Helen burst out. "No wonder Garrison seems totally goofy about her."

He does?

"Is he?" The detective turned to Lucinda and focused all attention on her. "How well do you know Mr. Prince?"

Oh, dear. Will he look guilty if I tell the detective that I didn't know—that I know him by another name?

"You must recall, Miss Ashton, that it is a crime to lie to the police or to withhold information that would aid in solving a crime—if it doesn't implicate you, of course. Fifth amendment."

"Oh, no. Nothing like that. But see, I don't know *Mr. Garrison Prince*. I know Gary Prinz, and while I imagine they're very similar people, I didn't know he was the actor until tonight."

"I think we all know why he didn't sign his contract now, don't we?" Claws out now, Helen eyed Lucinda with what could only be called disdain. "An actor not good enough for a cigarillo girl?"

"*Gary* just informed me of his intention of attending the Bible Institute of Los Angeles. I imagine *Garrison's* work would interfere with those classes, and that decided it for him." Only once the words danced off her tongue and onto the table did Lucinda realize how snappish they'd sounded.

Detective Lindstrom merely offered a smile that felt like approval. "I suspect you're correct if that is truly his plan. I'll ask him about it." Despite his saying so, Lucinda noted the man didn't write that down. His officer did, however. He continued. "While you're here, Miss Ashton, although we'll need a full statement from you in a bit, where were *you* when Miss Labelle—or rather, *Flint*—was shot?"

"Just at the front. I was heading down the aisle with my

tray. It scared me, and I used to go out hunting with the family. If a gun fired when we didn't see it, we dropped in case another hunter was out. I imagine instinct took over." At his look, one she couldn't categorize, Lucinda added, "I suppose that wouldn't have helped here unless someone took a second shot." *And why didn't I recognize it as a gunshot? Champagne cork, indeed!*

There Helen began screeching again, certain that she could have been next if the murderer tried again to get Gary. Lindstrom didn't bother asking Helen what she meant. Instead, he turned to Lucinda and, without a word, demanded to know.

"It's Miss Fenwick's opinion that whoever did this was trying to kill Gary—likely because of his unwillingness to sign that contract, although I don't understand that."

Sobbed, choked, and blubbered explanations followed, but the detective excused them, warning he might need to speak to them again. Just as the door started to close behind them, Lucinda heard him say, "I want to speak to this Prince fellow next."

FIVE

The moment the ladies disappeared through the side door at the back, a blast of hot air hit Garrison on the side of the face. “This is *your* doing, Prince! You’ve ruined me with your selfish money grubbing!” Stale tobacco and whisky mingled and assaulted his nostrils as the man continued. “I’ll pay up, of course, but what’ll I do for a leading lady now? Helen? Does she have what it takes?”

“I don’t know, sir,” Garrison began. “But you’ll have to find someone to take *my* place. I told you six months ago that I’d—”

He dodged a fist just in time. The nearest officer came to break up a “fight,” but when Garrison insisted that the man was just upset about the loss of a friend and employee, and Walker agreed, the officer let Walker go. Still, as he passed, Garrison couldn’t help but hear him mutter, “You’ll pay for this, Prince.”

Anyone who hadn’t heard about his defection from the Hollywood elite couldn’t have missed it now. Murmurs rippled over the room as people speculated, and questions fired at him, one after the other. After several harrowing minutes, a young woman, tallish, slender, bobbed and Marceled hair, and those ridiculous beads swaying with each step, sashayed over to him. With one hand on his arm, she said, "Garrison, the most vicious rumors are circulating."

He stared at her hand until the wo—no, she was another child masquerading as someone older. Until the *girl* released his arm with a blush. The impatience that flitted through her features suggested she knew she blushed, and it annoyed her. *Good. You've not lost all sense of propriety yet.*

The flirting did not stop. "Perhaps if you give me a hint about your next picture, I can counteract the rumors."

"There won't be another picture, Miss..."

"Smith. Opal Smith." Her smile showed perfect pearly teeth but never reached her eyes. In an undertone she murmured, "This is a brilliant publicity stunt of Walker's. It's creating a sensation. I'm just trying to help. I'm on the short list for *Broadway Revue*. With Miss Labelle's unfortunate accident, I should be called..."

If only your excitement didn't permeate every downcast look and sigh.

"I'll just leave a few well-timed hints that you might reconsider if the fans made enough of a to-do."

Before he could stop her, Miss Opal Smith turned heel and sashayed back from whence she'd come. A second glance showed her chatting with a dark-haired, ruby-lipped little Mary Pickford type. Something about the girl looked familiar, but his head was too muddled to consider what. *Why must every would-be actress in the country try to look like every other actress?*

When Walker shot a look his way, Garrison groaned. *He thinks I'm playing games.* In an attempt to quell any further complications, he shook his head the next time Walker looked his way. A scowl formed on the man's face, and he broke through a crowd and toward the back exit. Miss Smith followed.

Resigned, Garrison thanked those closest who had kind things to say about his acting and strolled down the far-right aisle toward the same exit. He'd have to make it clear—bring up his lawyer, even—before Walker found some way to use it against him. *Before he figures out who Cinda is and bullies her.*

Just as he neared the end of the aisle, the door opened and Cinda led a weeping Helen out. He waved and hurried to meet them.

Crack!

Screams pierced the room. Shouts followed. Policemen ran, but Garrison ran faster as both girls slowly slumped to the floor. "Cinda!"

At the same moment Lucinda heard a second *crack,* Helen gasped and slumped against her. Unprepared, the girl's weight pulled both of them to the floor. Gasping, struggling, Helen clung to her until… nothing. Glassy-eyed, she stared off into space as Gary pulled her from Lucinda's grasp.

"Is she—?"

"Gone, I think," Lucinda whispered. Tears filled her eyes as tremors rippled over her. *It could have been me.*

Guilt would have settled in, but Gary lifted Helen and followed a police officer while a short, thickset woman helped her to her feet. "You come with me."

"I—" She gazed after Gary, but the woman led her in the opposite direction.

"You need to clean up, my dear."

"Clean?" A glance down at her clothes showed a spray of blood across her crisp, white shirt. "Oh…"

A familiar scene played out before her as the woman argued with the officer about allowing her to wash. "She's an employee here. They cannot have her wandering about dripping in blood, sir."

"Well, may that be as it is," the fellow began, "we have two murders to concern ourselves with."

As the words tried to arrange themselves into sensible

order in Lucinda's mind, she stared at her hands, touched her face, her hair. When she then saw blood smeared all over them, she nearly retched. That seemed to change the man's tune.

"Of course, of course. I'll be timing you. Five minutes at most."

"We'll take however long we need to clean her up, and your superior will hear from my husband about this."

At the ladies' washroom, the woman checked to see that it was empty before leading Lucinda inside. "What a lot of bumbledom," she muttered.

"If I'd been shot," Lucinda began with more confusion than deliberate hesitation, "I would feel it, wouldn't I? Surely some sort of pain?"

Alarm filled the woman's features as she began helping Lucinda out of the tuxedo jacket. "You think you were hit?"

"I'm so confused, that I wondered."

"You're trembling… shock, perhaps?" The woman rolled up her sleeves and urged her to wash the hands. "I'll wet a towel. What confuses you?"

"Some of the things the officer said—"

Laughter reverberated against the walls around them. "'May that be as it is?' First time I've heard that order. He's trying to sound important and only made a fool of himself."

At first, scrubbing only spread the blood further. Hands trembling, heart racing, stomach churning, she rolled the bar of soap over and over in her hands. It turned pink. Lucinda gagged.

"I'm sorry…"

"Don't be. This isn't your fault at all."

A good look at the woman showed a thin line of dark hair along her upper lip. Kind eyes belied the tight, pursed lips and the set of her jaw. Silver streaks through Marceled waves showed both a nod to fashion and one to comfort with aging.

So many middle-aged women had taken to dyeing their hair to hide the gray.

"She really is dead, isn't she?"

"I'm afraid so."

Lucinda scrubbed harder. "Perhaps the first shot wasn't meant for Gary, then."

"Garrison Prince? They think Miss Labelle was killed by mistake?"

As she raised her head to look in the mirror above the sink, the woman turned her head. "Don't look, Miss…?"

"Ashton. Lucinda Ashton." She'd forgotten about the blood on Helen's face. *I must have it, too.*

"You don't want to see. I'm Mrs. Cohen, and I don't think you can be so certain about Mr. Prince's safety. We must hurry." The woman worked to rid Lucinda's face of any traces of blood as she spoke. "I saw the whole thing, and it definitely could have been meant for Mr. Prince if it came from where I think it did."

Lucinda grabbed the woman's arm and looked her square in the eye. "Did you *see* the shooter?"

"I saw the curtain ripple when I looked for a shooter."

Another swipe of the cloth followed, but Lucinda didn't have time for that. If Gary was the target, his would-be murderer had missed. Again. She turned the tap on full blast and cupped her hands beneath it. Over and over she rubbed and splashed until Mrs. Cohen declared her face and hair blood-free.

"Would you ask the officer if someone may retrieve a clean shirt for me?" I don't think my employer would appreciate me walking around drenched in blood." Lucinda amended that statement. "That is, he would see it that way, even if it is just blotches."

"I'll be right back. Lock the door behind me."

Lucinda never would have thought of that. Realizing why the woman had said it, Lucinda sank onto the low bench by the mirror and tried to calm zinging nerves. A glance at herself showed her hair a mess, her clothes even messier. *Once Gary sees me, I'll know if he loves me or if he thinks he loves a pretty face. A "true beauty" he called me. I wonder what he'll say to messy, stringy hair or worse, frizzes and wild?*

That was all it took. While she waited for Mrs. Cohen to return with a fresh shirt, she unpinned her hair, braided the front pieces to get them out of the way, and pinned it all up again. A good look in the mirror showed her looking much better, aside from the blood staining her shirt.

"Stains!" She unbuttoned as quickly as possible and began working the blood out, bit by bit. Shirt done, she removed her slip, washed it out, and even dabbed at the faint spots on her brassiere. Her corset had made it unscathed.

By the time the woman knocked on the door, she'd managed to get the worst of the blood off the black jacket. No one would notice. "I've returned, Miss Ashton."

Lucinda rushed to open the door. She hid behind it as the woman entered. "I'll leave off my slip," she explained as she pulled on the shirt. "And the jacket will cover enough. Thank you ever so much."

"Very sensible. I saw officers speaking with your Mr. Prince. Let's hurry."

ONLY AFTER BEING LED toward the exit doors and him glancing back to see Cinda exiting out the front did Garrison realize that someone had let about half the room leave. *Well done. Quietly. One by one, I imagine. No overreactions and panicked demands to go, too.*

"Just this way, sir. Detective Lindstrom has questions for you."

Before they could open the doors, shouts from backstage sent his escort rushing back. "Stay here, sir."

Instinct said to follow—to help. Not obeying orders from the police, however—it went against everything he'd ever been taught. But which was more important *this* time?

A few more shouts followed—still indistinct, but Garrison heard a couple of words clearly. Find. Gone. A foul word ripped through the entire theater, followed by someone getting a berating.

At least they care, I suppose.

He waited, feeling every eye on him as he stood there. *Odd that I'm never uncomfortable with it on set, but…*

Another officer approached. "Mr. Prince? The detective is ready for you now."

"Everything all right?"

Not until the door closed behind them did the man say, "Someone thought they saw someone move—probably wishful thinking. There wasn't anyone there."

From behind a door, a man yelled at someone for the inappropriate use of unsavory language. The officer led Garrison past and murmured, "I hope no one out front heard…"

"They did—almost everyone, I imagine."

"Gregg's in trouble, then. Hope O'Grady doesn't find out or…" The man paused and knocked before entering what looked to be the stockroom for the candy and cigarettes.

Couldn't they have given him an office?

"Mr. Prince?" The detective didn't rise. "Please have a seat. I'm Detective Lindstrom." He shot out a hand as he added, "Are you all right?"

Garrison grasped it and shook before sitting down. "Yes—but Helen…"

The man nodded. "My men are searching everywhere, but I decided I needed to talk to you, and now again to Miss Ashton, before I join them. The first shot could have been caused by anything, but a second implies more. Do you know any reason someone would want to kill the ladies of Imperial Studios?"

"I—" Garrison blinked. "Well, I hadn't thought of it that way. At first, we assumed I was the real target. I've…"

"Made a few enemies today, from what I've heard," Lindstrom said. "But with two women dead…" He picked up a paper, scanned it, and set it down again. "Who did you arrive with this evening?"

"Eva—Miss Labelle." When the man waited, ostensibly for more, Garrison added, "We came in the same car, faced the reporters together, and after some mingling, seated ourselves in our reserved seats. Helen is—" He swallowed hard. "That is, *was* to have a much larger role in Imperial's next picture, so she was seated with us."

"Was anyone else seated *with* you?"

"No…" He tried to recall who else had been in their row. "I think a couple of the other girls were on the other side of Helen, but I don't remember seeing them after the shot."

Lindstrom pointed at someone in the back and said, "Find out." Without looking back at Garrison, he scribbled something on his paper while asking, "And what next?"

"Well, the movie played, it came to the intermiss—no. No, that's not right."

There Lindstrom looked up, pencil poised. "What isn't?" He glanced down at the paper and back up again.

"I meant that I forgot something in there. Cinda and the other girls came up the aisles after we were seated. Eva wanted cigarettes, and I asked for Goobers."

That earned him a sharp look. "Wouldn't have taken you for a candy fellow."

"I'm not. My sweet tooth runs to baked goods—pies, cakes, cookies…"

"But you purchased the candy…?"

He felt his neck heating, but Garrison answered frankly. "I always order something from Cinda, and she only sells cigarettes and candy."

"You don't smoke, Mr. Prince?"

He shook his head, and at the man's continued questioning gaze, added, "At first I just didn't like it—couldn't afford to develop a habit for something frivolous. Later I..." Garrison didn't know what to say. Everything that came to mind sounded arrogant at best and more likely, self-righteous.

"It may seem to you like these questions can't possibly help us find who killed these two young ladies, but I assure you that I need every bit of seemingly trivial information from which to see patterns."

"It's just that I became a Christian, sir."

"I consider myself one, although I indulge in a cigar from time to time."

Did he hear an edge to the detective's tone? Garrison couldn't decide. He plunged on with his explanation. "For me, it was a relief—one thing I didn't have to examine in Scripture to see if it belonged in my life. For now, Volstead has made the need to study about alcoholic consumption unnecessary."

"Is this spiritual awakening the reason behind your decision not to continue with Imperial Studios?"

"Somewhat, sir." How could he explain without sounding even more pompous and affected? "I would have left anyway, even if I had not yielded to the call of Christ, after I—"

The door burst open, and an officer dragged a young man into the room. "Found this fella with a casing in his hand."

Garrison was ignored as Lindstrom rose and in one fluid movement, pulled out a handkerchief to accept the casing. "Take him into another room and begin questioning. I'll be there shortly."

Then, as if nothing had interrupted them, he turned back to Garrison and said, "You were saying that even if you hadn't had a spiritual change of heart, you would have..."

"I'd met a young lady. I've seen what this business does to relationships." He tried to meet the detective's gaze and failed. "I knew quickly that unless something came up to change my mind, I'd want to marry her."

"And this lady's name is…"

He stared at his hands, noting that one of his nails had chipped. The stagehands would never scold him for that again. The detective leaned forward. "Mr. Prince, may I remind you that this is a *murder* investigation?"

"I'm aware of that," he responded. "However, what I have to say is something I haven't—that is, my girl doesn't—I mean —" *Could you sound more like a rube?*

"As I am unlikely to have to speak to her about anything regarding your matrimonial plans…" When Garrison looked up, the man offered a tight smile. "In fact, I'm not likely to speak to her at all."

"You already have."

The man scanned the paper. When that didn't satisfy him, he reached back for the officer's notebook and scanned it, too. "I don't see…" The words trailed off as Detective Lindstrom began to nod. "You mentioned Cinda. I presume you mean Miss Lucinda Ashton?"

"Yes, sir."

"She appears to have a good head on her shoulders."

Is this where I say, "Thank you?" For what? My good taste?

"And she doesn't know of your matrimonial plans?"

Miserable, he slumped in the chair. "I've made it plain that I have every intention of proposing on Sunday. I'd have done it tomorrow, but she has to work tomorrow night." Once he began, Garrison found it difficult not to spill all. "My contract isn't up until midnight, you see, and I wanted to be just Gary Prinz again before I asked—that's all she knew me as, although I tried to get her to notice me after a time. Most of the girls here don't do that—pay undue attention to the actors and actresses. Not if they want to keep their jobs."

"She didn't know she was walking out with *the* Garrison Prince?"

"Hard to believe, but no. And now that she's found out this way, I don't know…"

A knock startled Garrison into sitting bolt upright. Detective Lindstrom ordered whoever it was to enter. A small officer with an apologetic look poked his head into the room, but a moment later, he stumbled forward as a large woman—Miriam Cohen, no less—pushed past the man, dragging Cinda behind her.

"I believe Mr. Prince is still in danger!"

Ignoring the detective's irritated huff, Garrison rose and went to Cinda. "Are you all right?"

Never had he imagined that he'd be thrilled to have a woman burst into tears, but when he pulled her into his arms and she clung to him, thrilled was the best word to describe his elation. *She doesn't hate me yet.*

SIX

"I saw the shooting, detective, and with what Miss Ashton has shared with me—"

"Excuse me, ma'am, but who are you and why have you barged in—?"

"Because," Mrs. Cohen continued without apologizing for her interruption, "*this man…*" She pointed at Gary. "He may still be in danger."

Lucinda heard every word and each one should have made sense, but really, they didn't. At least the steady *thrum, thrum* of Gary's heart beneath her ear slowly beat away her fear. He'd murmured something—something she'd missed. Then the words reassembled themselves in her mind. "It'll be all right, Cinda. Trust me. Trust the Lord," he'd whispered.

Detective Lindstrom stood and pointed to the officer who hadn't kept them out of the room. "Get back to your post and don't let this happen again."

"Sorry, sir."

The moment the door shut behind him, Mrs. Cohen turned a haughty glare on the detective. "You can't blame him. He wouldn't have kept me out without manhandling me, which thankfully he didn't attempt to do. I'd have sued the department and won, and you know it."

"Who are you?"

"Miriam Cohen," she answered with a huff. "And—"

"Mrs. *Cohen*," the man began with ill-disguised exasperation. "I'm investigating a *murder*—"

"Yes, and I'm trying to help you prevent *another* one. If what I saw is what I think, then the shooter may have been aiming for Mr. Prince after all." She shot a look at Gary. "Sunset Studios would love to talk to you about a contract, Mr. Prince." Without missing a beat, she continued. "I saw the curtain ripple, and where it was, I think the gun could have been aimed at Mr. Prince, and the girls got in the way."

Detective Lindstrom seated himself and *looked* at the woman. "And, if you don't mind the impertinence of my asking, what makes you confident in your ability to know the specific trajectory of a bullet based on a curtain ripple?"

"I can't, of course." She jerked an empty chair over and plopped into it, her hands clenched in her lap. "But I've been on set enough with these sorts of things." She tossed Gary another smile. "I like to understand what my husband's company does." Turning back to the detective who, in Lucinda's estimation, had begun to look amused, she added, "Of course, the pistol—I assume it *was* a pistol?"

"Ma'am—"

"Whatever. Pistol or rifle, the barrel can be pointed in any direction, but since Mr. Garrison was near the victim both times and has had death threats today, one should not risk his life again by making assumptions."

No one spoke a word. Lucinda opened her eyes and seeing blood on Gary's shirt averted them to the nearby shelves. Charleston Chews, Wrigley's chewing gums, several kinds of cigarettes and more candy. Candy… Why did that thought bother her?

"Cinda?"

She glanced up and saw concern in Gary's expression. "Hmm?"

"What is it?"

Looking around, she saw everyone staring at them. "I—" That was the trouble. She didn't know what had bothered her, and now with everyone staring, she couldn't remember at all. "I don't know."

A kerfuffle outside the door prompted a scowl. Detective Lindstrom shot a look at the man behind him and turned back to Mrs. Cohen. "I—"

The door burst open, and the officer said, "Sir, the folks out in the theater are gettin' awfully restless. This one just came in to say they're all leaving—not him, of course, or he wouldn't have come in, but—"

"They're not going anywhere." Lindstrom rose and shot a weary look at Lucinda, Gary, and Mrs. Cohen. "You three go back to the theater and keep quiet about your theories. I'll call you back as soon as I can. If it weren't for all these interruptions, I might be through with this part of the investigation!"

He spoke as if shouting, but the man's volume never raised above conversational levels. With Gary's arm around her shoulder, and Mrs. Cohen right beside her, they made their way back into the theater. Only a third of the people were left. The balcony area had been emptied and was now dark. The orchestra pit had been emptied and all instruments put away. A glance at the organ showed the organist gone.

"He'd been playing, so it couldn't be him," she mused aloud.

"What was that?"

Lucinda pointed to the enormous Wurlitzer organ, but the words didn't come. Gary steered her that way, and Mrs. Cohen followed. "I think shock is settling in. After all, she was reasonably close to two gunshots today."

Her mind insisted that she knew what those words meant, but even as she walked across the richly patterned carpet,

Lucinda tried to follow them. A cigarette butt, still smoldering, lay on the carpet. She broke away from Gary and snatched it up. After licking her fingers, she squeezed it a few quick times before it finally went out. "Smokers are so inconsiderate," she snapped.

Tears flowed then. Gary pulled her close once more and led her to the organ. He seated her and offered to find a glass of water. "Perhaps some coffee?"

"They won't allow that," Mrs. Cohen snapped. "But you stay with her. I'll see what *I* can do."

Alone with Gary, Lucinda grew nervous and turned to face the organ. One hand resting on the bench, the other on the keys, she tried to imagine what it might be like to know which ones to press to make the sounds needed for the perfect melody. Music sat resting on the rack, the black notes marching up and down the lines like ants working their way through a picnic.

"I wish I could play."

"We'll get you lessons," Gary assured her.

When we're married? Will that ever happen?

When Lucinda didn't respond, he lowered himself to the bench beside her and murmured, "Please don't be angry with me, Cinda."

"You didn't tell me who you were. Why?"

"I—"

She interrupted him as what Mrs. Cohen had said finally reached the proper connections in her brain. "Gary!"

He stiffened and made a move to push her down, but she wrenched herself from his grasp. Staring at him, she gasped, "Mrs. Cohen!"

"She couldn't have done it, Cinda. I—"

"No!" Startled by her own vehemence, Lucinda lowered her voice and leaned closer to him. "What she said. It's true. The first time I was close enough that, depending on where the shooter was, the shot could have been meant for me, and the second time, I was right there. Not even inches away."

Eyes closed, doing everything she could to steady nerves that wanted to send her into hysterics, she said, "What if the bullets were meant for me?"

THE OPULENCE of the Taj Mahal Theater intruded on their quiet corner even before Mrs. Cohen returned with the glass of water and candy bar. She listened to Lucinda's concerns with the eyes of one who saw more than was spoken. "I'll return after I speak with Mr. Cohen. Perhaps he'll be able to make that detective listen." She eyed Garrison with a hard look. "You'll protect her?"

"I will." Though he didn't speak it, his heart insisted, *With my life.*

The woman's smile told him that, again, she heard what he didn't say.

As she strode away with a tread that looked more suited to sturdy boots than evening shoes, Lucinda leaned against his arm, froze, and relaxed, her head resting on his shoulder. "Gary…?"

"Yes?"

"I know that you want to wait until Sunday to talk about this, but I don't know if I'll be there Sunday if I don't know the answer to one question."

His heart clenched. "Cinda, I did try to tell you—not in our times at the park, but on nights when you sold me cigarettes and candy." He gazed out over the theater, his eyes taking in the repetitious patterns, the gilt edges, the marble statues of Indian gods and goddesses. The gold velvet seats. The arches.

"If you'd said my name…"

Again, he hesitated before saying, "I did tonight when I

tipped you. You never looked at me. Not once."

"It's recommended that we don't. If we fawn over the actors and actresses, we could lose our jobs." She met his gaze and held it. "But all the times we walked through the park, the times we ate at the lunch counter after church, or the times we went to the *pictures* at Tally's… why not tell me then?"

Prayer was his only hope. *Well, the One who answers prayer is. How can I explain without casting doubt on her character?*

"Gary?"

"Can you imagine, for just a moment, that all you do is serve people candy and cigarettes? You go home, walk into Mrs. Smith's parlor, and she says, 'I'd like some Chesterfields, please.'" He smiled at her wrinkled nose but continued. "And when you went into the drug store to have a malted, how would you feel if someone stopped you on the way and asked for a package of chewing gum? You enter church, and the minister requests you see what everyone would like before he begins his sermon." He covered their hands with his other and said, "How would you like your whole life to be nothing but what you saw as a means to support yourself?"

She watched him, her eyes searching for something he hoped she found… or didn't. Which was it?

"I don't like the sound of it," she said after a long pause. "But can you see why I don't know who you are? Are you Garrison Prince the Hollywood star, or are you Gary Prinz —*my* Gary, who likes my new green dress—all covered in dust and cobwebs now—better than my pink one?"

"Which one did I choose today when I refused to sign a contract?" he countered. "Cinda, I told Mr. Walker that I wouldn't sign six months ago. I decided even before that—before I met you, but once I did meet you, I knew I wouldn't be tempted to change my mind no matter what he offered."

"Is he really so very angry?"

"Furious. He threatened me, but I thought it was embarrassment talking. He'd called in the press for the contract signing. I think he assumed I wouldn't make a scene, and he'd have me for another six years."

She took her hand from his, smoothed her skirt, laced her fingers together, and rested them on her lap, but she didn't move from his side. "I think I understand—somewhat. You didn't know if I'd be like the Smith girls."

Only when he saw himself staring down at her did Garrison realize he had stood—probably paced a bit, too. "You don't understand. I didn't think about what you'd do—not after the first couple of days, anyway. I just enjoyed being Gary again." He forced himself to sit down again as he said, "I just enjoyed being *me* with you."

His hopes plummeted as she shook her head. "I don't understand." Cinda gave him a weak smile. "But I have a couple of days to work on it, don't I?"

"You're still coming on Sunday?"

A *bang!* rang out from backstage. Gary dove for her, pinning her down. Screams rippled through the theater again. He heard footsteps pounding up the stairs, and an officer pushed open the curtain. "Sorry folks," he shouted to the room. "Someone knocked over a flat board. No one's hurt."

Standing, he offered his hand and helped Cinda to her feet. She gave him a wobbly smile and said, "I'm coming unless we die here first." As if speaking the words drove home all that had happened, Lucinda Ashton burst into tears.

For one melodramatic moment, Lucinda allowed herself to think, *If I can't trust Gary, I hope we do die here.* Then she rose, brushed off her skirt and smoothed her hair, scolding herself all the while. *I do* not *wish to die rather than lose Gary, but if I had any lingering doubts about my affection for him…* Lucinda paused her thoughts and listened to her heart before continuing. *I think they're gone. Now I have to decide if his duality equals inexcusable duplicity… but after I sleep.*

"Cinda, are you all right? You look… dazed." Gary's words wrapped her in concern and held her close, even as he made a visible effort to hold himself back.

"Just…" She closed her eyes, steadied herself, and tried again. "So much to take in."

Gary tried to urge her to sit again. "It's hard to imagine that someone in this room is a murderer." The moment the words left his lips, he apologized. "I don't know what I was thinking bringing that up. You've been through enough without—"

Mrs. Cohen appeared and began scolding both of them—Gary for not insisting she drink the water and eat the candy bar, Lucinda for not doing it in the first place. "Now I want a good long drink out of you before another word."

"No." Lucinda ignored her for a moment and turned back to Gary. "You're wrong. The shooter may not be in this room. After all, he wasn't in here when he fired the gun. He could have left by the back door, hidden somewhere, come in and mingled, or a host of other ideas, but there's no guarantee he's out here, considering both shots appear to have come from back there."

With the glass now thrust into her hand, Lucinda drank as Mrs. Cohen relayed what her husband had learned. "They're letting almost everyone else go," she said. "Everyone who has someone who can verify his or her presence during both shots." After a pointed look that prompted Lucinda to take another sip of water, she added, "I believe both of you will be allowed to leave since you couldn't have been the shooter. They'll speak with you tomorrow."

"I can't—" Lucinda stopped mid-thought. "I—that is…" More nonsensical words babbled as she watched a girl chatting with Mr. Walker—*flirting* it seemed. "What is she—?"

Another girl slipped around the orchestra pit and through the left side door. *Was that…? No…*

"Lucinda?"

"Excuse me a moment." Lucinda thrust the water glass back into Mrs. Cohen's hands and dashed to follow.

Gary would have come, too, but she firmly pushed the door closed in his face saying, "Stay out there. Someone back here could be out to harm you."

"But—"

The door had a lock, and Lucinda utilized it. A single pound and a "Cinda! No!" followed, but she ignored it and went to see what Opal thought she was doing behind stage with a murderer on the loose. *Foolish girl.* The fact that she'd gone into the fray as well did not speak much for her own intelligence, but Lucinda chose to ignore that bit of information.

Officers swarmed the area, but Lucinda managed to dodge most of them. Oddly enough, Opal appeared to have done so as well. She couldn't find the girl anywhere, and not one officer led anyone out to the front of the house.

The third time she barely managed to dodge an oncoming policeman, Lucinda decided it wasn't worth getting into trouble to save Opal from self-inflicted foolishness. *She should have looked to the consequences… as should have I.*

A hand grabbed her arm just as Lucinda slipped back through the door and into the theater. A man's hand. She jumped, wrenching her arm from the grasp and ready to run.

"Cinda!"

"You startled me!"

Mrs. Cohen appeared at her other elbow. "Whatever made you go back there?"

"I thought I saw—"

The lights flickered. All eyes rose to the great chandeliers overhead, to the lights in the sconces along the walls, and to the stage area. A *bang!* rang out through the back of the theater. A few bulbs popped. The entire room plunged into darkness.

She felt Gary move closer, put his arm around her shoulder. He asked if she was all right before asking Mrs. Cohen the same. "Was it another shot?"

"More likely the fuse box," Mrs. Cohen said. "It's not uncommon for them have an explosion of sorts, and it didn't sound the same as those shots did to me." The woman's voice was nearer, as if she'd turned to Lucinda. "What do you think, Miss Ashton?"

"I agree. It sounded much less sharp—less of a crack and more of a bang." Tears threatened, but Lucinda did everything she could to hide them. As Gary's arm tightened around her, she realized she hadn't succeeded. One tear rolled down her cheek followed by another and then… more than she could count.

Grateful for the cover of darkness, she waited for the ushers to appear. The doors swung open. Beams of light entered. Gary turned her toward them. "Let's go up top and see if they'll let us go. I'll take you back to Mrs. Smith's—"

"I can't go back there tonight."

Just as they reached the aisle, the side door opened, and two officers emerged, supporting someone in the middle. As an usher neared, they saw him—Detective Lindstrom. Hunched over, the man gripped his side and allowed himself to be half-pushed, half-carried along. Gary spoke the words first.

"I suppose it was a gunshot. Just fired from a different place?"

Mrs. Cohen moved closer to Lucinda and murmured, "Stay close together, and I'm coming up the rear. If either of you are targets, we're all sitting ducks."

At the back doors, the officers wouldn't let anyone leave. "Someone shot Detective Lindstrom, and we're—" a few reckless expletives flew from the man's mouth. As annoyed as she might usually have been, Lucinda ignored the words.

"We couldn't have shot him if we were up here," Mrs. Cohen argued.

"Until the detective's safe and we have searched for the gunman, no one leaves," the man argued. "Just take your seats, and we'll be with you as soon as we can."

A roomful of silhouettes stood about, talking, complaining, crying. A tall, thin man moved to where Gary, Lucinda, and Mrs. Cohen stood and said, "I'm trying, Miriam, but you see how they are."

"If either of these people die because the police can't do their jobs…"

What else the couple said, Lucinda didn't hear. Something was wrong, terribly wrong, but her mind refused to cooperate and reason out a solution. Her nose, however, did. "Do I smell… smoke?"

SEVEN

Someone heard Cinda's question and repeated it—loudly. A scream erupted, and Garrison could have sworn Cinda said, "That sounds like Ruby."

A girl rushed for the stage. Another followed, as if back shadows of silhouettes across a dimly lit screen. A few officers raced after them. A couple of ushers followed, trying to keep their little flashlights trained ahead of the running policemen.

One tripped. His flashlight flew ahead of him and crashed to the ground. Whether the fall killed it, or it rolled out of sight, Garrison couldn't tell. Panicked people raced in all directions as the distinct smell of smoke became unmistakable.

Garrison saw what he thought was an unguarded door and herded their little group that way. "Shh… keep low, but come with me. We're getting out of here."

At the stage area, people began coughing. If that meant what he thought it did, they'd converge on the front doors now. "Hurry!"

Mrs. Cohen stopped, and he nearly attempted to lift and carry her, but a moment later, she trudged on, and something whacked his leg. *Did she really take off her shoes?*

Once in the lobby, the pishtaq-shaped windows showed

which way out, but a push to the door yielded nothing. "Locked." He turned to Cinda, who hadn't left his side. "Where is an exit the officers might not have bothered to lock?"

"The eastern vestibule has one—for fires. It's never supposed to be locked if anyone is inside. Like the back doors." A half-choked sob followed. "And the front."

"Well, let's try it. Hurry, before we get trampled." He fumbled for her hand and pulled her alongside him. "This way?"

"Yes…"

They fumbled, walking as quickly as possible in almost total darkness. He felt along the wall as they went, trying not to knock off paintings or stumble over furniture. The beautiful decor he'd always admired suddenly felt unnecessary and a hindrance.

"It should be on the other wall," Cinda whispered as voices filled the passageway behind them. "Any time now."

Garrison urged the other three to hold onto each other and said, "Stay together. I'll find the knob."

People surged toward them, screaming, whimpering, crying, coughing. Gary felt all over the wall, frantic to find a doorway before being trampled by the others or worse, restrained by the police. *Surely with smoke they'd let us out… wouldn't they?*

He felt molding—a doorjamb. It took several more seconds, but there was the knob. Locked. He rammed the door with his shoulder, but nothing happened. More people screamed. He kicked at the door and thought he heard something crack. Two more kicks, another ram, Mr. Cohen joining him, and they stumbled out into the night and landed on the ground. Gravel ripped into his hands and forearms, but Garrison didn't care.

Illogically, he glanced at his watch with the luminescent numbers and hands—a gift from the studio. Two minutes after midnight. "I'm Gary Prinz again," he murmured to himself.

Cinda appeared at his elbow and helped him up. "Hurry. Out of the way."

As they backed away from the building, the first flame appeared from near the back. Screams followed, and people rushed away from the building. Mrs. Cohen asked about their car. Mr. Cohen said they'd have a difficult time finding their driver at that time of night.

"We'll have to find a taxi."

"Not in this crush," Cinda muttered.

But Gary had an idea. "Come with me…" He took off toward the back of the building. "We'll go to Franklin and call from the all-night diner over there. Everyone else will head to Sunset, I'm sure."

Mr. Cohen insisted they wait until his wife could put on her shoes again. "I don't have to run anymore," she said. "And I'm too large to expect to be able not to break an ankle trying to run in these things."

"We'll get a taxi," Gary insisted, "and take Cinda home first. She lives close—"

"No, Gary. I can't go back there."

What she said didn't bother him as much as her tone. "Why not?"

"It's a long story, but the end is that Mrs. Smith locked me in the cellar when I wouldn't agree to sneak the girls into the theater tonight. I *can't* go back until tomorrow, and then only to gather my things and leave!"

AFTER MRS. COHEN stepped in and stopped an interrogation worthy of the detective, both men managed to keep their questions to themselves for far longer than Lucinda might have expected. All along the trek to the diner, all while they waited for a car, all the long ride home to the Cohen's mansion in Beverly Hills, they talked. Gary hung over the front seat, twisted awkwardly so he could speak to her, wedged between the Cohens in the back.

First Mr. Cohen described the influx of actors and actresses who were flocking to Beverly Hills, and then Mrs. Cohen pointed out Pickfair as they passed the already famous estate and described several pieces of land her husband owned. Gary pointed at one. "I bought that lot back when the debate over annexation into Los Angeles was hot. It was a gamble and took every penny I had saved from my first contract, but I thought if Pickford, Fairbanks, and Valentino got their way, this area would boom."

"Property values are skyrocketing. Hold onto it for twenty years, boy. You'll make a bundle," Mr. Cohen advised.

He owns land up here, is buying a house in Pasadena, and just bought that car! He's done well for himself…

As if Mr. Cohen had peeked into her thoughts, he said, "Isn't that one next to it the one that Czech botanist built? I hear the gardens are going to be exquisite when they mature a bit."

"They are already," Gary said. "Mr. Vavra has taken me over some of it when I've gone to inspect my measly three acres."

"Three acres!" Lucinda couldn't help herself. "That must have cost heaps!"

Under her breath, Mrs. Cohen murmured, "Probably fifteen to twenty."

Only when they turned onto another street and slowed before a well-lit entrance did Lucinda realize the woman meant thousands. *Oh, my… But surely without a job, he wouldn't buy something so expensive in Pasadena… would he? The Oak Knoll house can't be more than a few thousand, surely.*

The wide drive into the Cohen estate took them through enormous wrought-iron gates. The lights at the front of the mansion alluded to its size, but as the taxi pulled up to a portico, Lucinda allowed her thoughts to release a silent whistle. *This is luxury!*

A butler or something of the sort met them at the door, his genteel English accent lending even more richness to the atmosphere. "Will there be refreshments, madame?"

"Let's have cocoa, Jervis. And perhaps a few sandwiches if you can manage. I don't think our Miss Ashton has had anything to eat in far too long."

As if to confirm the assertion, Lucinda's stomach rumbled. "I am famished, if it isn't too much trouble," she told the man.

"No trouble at all, miss." With a pointed look at Mr. Cohen, the man said, "Will there be anything else, sir?"

Their host said not, but when the man left, Gary urged him to have whatever he liked. "What you do in your home isn't my concern, sir."

Mrs. Cohen patted her husband's hand and spoke for him as they seated themselves in chairs side by side. She gestured for Lucinda and Gary to take seats on a long, velvet, tufted sofa. "Your courtesy only inspires ours, Mr. Prince."

At least, that's what Lucinda thought she'd said. One moment, she'd been listening, and the next Gary shook her awake. "There are sandwiches, Cinda. Eat a few and then get some sleep. You're beat."

Cheeks burning, Lucinda sat upright and nearly knocked the delicate plate from Gary's hands. "Oh, I'm so sorry." Her chagrin shifted to snappishness when she realized she'd slept against his shoulder. "You could have woken me before I made a fool of myself," she hissed.

That, of course, only made her feel worse as she saw the words strike him with the force of a physical blow. "I'm sorry, Gary. I'm tired, and—" Tears threatened, and the irritation inched its way into the rest of her apology, "—you…"

Don't blame him for your rudeness. It's not his fault.

After a sip or two of cocoa and Lucinda managing to

devour a sandwich before yawning again, Mrs. Cohen stood. "I think I'll show Lucinda to her room and find her something to sleep in." She smiled down at her husband as the man struggled to his feet. "Why don't you call the police and tell them where Lucinda and…?" A glance at Gary and back to Mr. Cohen. "Perhaps we should insist on Mr. Prince—"

"Gary, please. Just Gary Prinz now. Finally," he added as if relieved.

"Yes. Why don't we put him in the east room? Then we can all try to figure out what happened tonight over breakfast?" She turned to Gary. "You will stay, won't you, Gary? We enjoy guests, and we'd all be in one place when they assign someone new to the case."

That caught Lucinda's attention. "You think they'll want to ask us more questions? I don't see how it could help. We don't know anything…" She shot Gary a look. "Do we?" That's when she realized he'd risen, too, and had offered her a hand.

"Detective stories always say that people know more than they realize, so possibly, but I can't see what. We'll look it all over in the morning."

The look he gave her suggested that, had they been alone, he'd have kissed her—really kissed her this time. Resentment bubbled up until a yawn drove it away again. *I'd rather be alert when he finally does. And wasn't I not so confident of the wisdom of marrying a man so duplicitous?* Her brain shriveled as she tried to work out that idea. *Or did I decide something else?*

"Are you all right, Cinda?"

"Am I?" Those foolish tears reappeared. "I don't know."

With a quick squeeze of her hand, a promise to pray for her before he went to sleep, and assurances that he'd be there when she awoke, Gary allowed Mrs. Cohen to lead her away. As they turned to pass out of sight of the room, she glanced back to find him still there. Still watching.

"Oscar used to look at me like that—still does sometimes. He's a good man, your Gary."

"Is he?" Lucinda caught the swift look Mrs. Cohen shot her and sighed. "I can't remember. All I can think about is that he never told me who he really was."

Only once Mrs. Cohen nudged her into a bathroom and began running a steaming bath did the woman respond to that. "I would have imagined he thought he showed you who he really was until he didn't have to pretend to be someone else anymore."

While Mrs. Cohen busied herself finding towels and washcloths to give her guest privacy, Lucinda undressed as quickly as possible, slipped into the hot bath, and sank beneath an ever-growing pile of bubbles. "That sounds intelligent," she conceded. "I just can't think of why."

"We'll talk in the morning. You wash while I find you something to sleep in." She offered a reassuring smile and slipped out the door.

Hot, nearly scalding, water poured into the enormous tub and sent billows of jasmine and rose into the air. *If I don't just sleep right here in the tub…*

EIGHT

When Gary awoke for the third time and the room was still pitch black, he fumbled for his watch on the side table. The luminescent hands showed just past eight o'clock. The lightweight coverlet flung back with the sort of movement any director would appreciate in a scene but with the ease that made retakes simple for the actor, and Gary wondered if Mr. Cohen knew it. *Not your profession anymore*, one part of him argued. The other suggested that mentioning it wouldn't be out of line but rather a courtesy.

As he fumbled for the tiny pull chain on the small lamp by his bedside, Gary braced himself for the onslaught of light. It wasn't overbearing, but compared to the blackness of the room, it might have been. He slipped from the bed and shuffled across the floor, his toes sinking into carpeting so thick it felt like a fleece.

Drapes slid open with a jerk, and the sun streamed in, bathing the room in a golden glow. The "east room" lived up to its moniker, and for just the briefest of moments, Gary wondered if he'd made a mistake leaving such a lucrative business for what would become a job that kept them fed, housed, but not much more. *Is it wrong to pray that You bless my investments,*

Father? I kept out of speculation as advised. Only real property and gold. The house… a bit of cash for Lucinda to furnish it simply, and the rest stored for the inevitable rainy days… With her, it'll be enough.

Conscience poked him. *Forgive me, Lord.* You *are enough.*

As he turned away from the window, Gary saw the clothes he'd folded and left in a pile by his bed draped over the chair, now cleaned and pressed. The tuxedo jacket would be too much, but if he left off his tie and unbuttoned the shirt at the collar, he'd look only a bit overdressed. Maybe roll up the sleeves…

Stubble left his face shadowed, but a look in the adjoining bathroom showed shaving things, a brush, a toothbrush and powder—everything he could wish for. Gary removed the shirt again and made quick work of the early morning scruffiness. As he blotted his face dry, he examined it through new eyes. *She never noticed.*

While Gary wasn't so vain as to assume that Lucinda had eyes for no one but him, the realization that he'd met her just shortly after she'd been moved from matinees to evening performances and premieres brought hope. *It might mean something.*

Once dressed, and with his room as neat as possible, he hurried out to see if Lucinda had awakened. It wasn't likely—not with her getting to bed after one o'clock, but perhaps she was like him—a consistent riser no matter what time she'd gone to bed. He didn't know what room she'd been given and realized that lingering could leave her exposed to speculation by anyone who noticed.

The staircase was even more impressive as early morning light streamed in from a glass cupola overhead. Gary took it at a jog, scanning the area and listening for any sign of life about the place. The man, Jervis, appeared at the base of the steps almost out of thin air and wished him a good morning.

"Would you care for breakfast indoors or out on the terrace, Mr. Prince?"

"I—" How did he answer that without presuming too much?

"Mr. and Mrs. Cohen are not yet down, but they would wish you to make yourself comfortable, sir." When Gary still didn't answer, the man smiled. "Perhaps a bit of toast and coffee on the terrace until someone else is ready to join you?"

The solution: almost perfect. "And perhaps a piece of paper and a pencil? I need to make a few notes…"

"Of course, sir. The doors are just through there." He gestured through the large room they'd sat in the previous night and to the wide doors beyond. "I'll be out with your coffee in a moment."

By the time Mrs. Cohen arrived, he'd assembled quite a list of things he recalled from the previous evening. She took the chair beside him, the sun on her back, and asked if he needed a cardigan. "It's still a bit chilly this morning."

"I'm comfortable but thank you."

"Writing your first sermon?" At his quick look, she smiled. "I'm not mocking you. In fact, I envy your willingness to give up so much for… what is the reward, Mr. Prinz?"

The emphasis on the Z told him she'd accepted the decision, despite not agreeing with it. By way of mutual consideration, he told her about sleeping well and the ease with which he'd flung back the covers. "I think Mr. Cohen's directors might appreciate knowing where you purchased the coverlet. It has a decided flair to it. I could tell even in the darkness."

"I'll let him know, but don't think I don't realize you've avoided my question."

"Not at all," Gary assured her. "I didn't care to forget my impression once I knew you would likely not take offense at hearing it. As for my reward, I have it already—salvation. I know it isn't the done thing to talk about in society, but you asked. Some men are eager to share how to receive the Lord's gift. I wish to teach those who already have it how to live in a way that reflects their gratitude for it."

She seemed to wait for more, but Gary said nothing. He'd learned that those who wanted more would ask. Those who did not would rest easy when he didn't use the conversation as an opportunity to practice his sermon-giving skills. As usual, that moment while she waited and he said nothing stretched out awkwardly.

"And are there many unmarried preachers? Young ones, that is?"

"Not many," he said. "Although I hope not to be unmarried for long."

Though she didn't speak, Gary heard Mrs. Cohen's *And does Lucinda know about that?* clearly.

"I've not yet asked Cinda if she'll marry me. That was supposed to happen tomorrow. I hope it still may, but I wonder if maybe a bit of time to recover from something so distressing…"

"I suspect most young ladies would appreciate the diversion." Between sips of coffee, Mrs. Cohen added, "Are you practicing your proposal then?"

Though tempted to slide the paper across the table and allow her to figure it out for herself, with his deplorable penmanship, she'd never be able to read it. Instead, he read it aloud. "At intermission, one gunshot. Eva hit and died. Helen was there. I was there. Lucinda was not too far away. Mr. Walker sat in two rows ahead of us, toward the middle."

On and on he went, noting who had made or insinuated threats against him, where everyone had been, and even the girl who had glared at him. "She was a Pickford lookalike. Petite, dark hair, wide eyes—well, after she stopped scowling and smiled, anyway."

"I think I recall seeing someone like that—scarlet dress with black beading?"

"Yes." He might have said more, but Cinda appeared in a simple blue dress—a bit more chic than he was accustomed to seeing on her but flattering. Gary smiled as he rose and held a chair for her. "You look lovely this morning, Cinda."

There it was again, that half-startled look she'd given him… was it only yesterday?

"Thank you." She offered a quick smile that she just as quickly turned onto Mrs. Cohen. "Good morning."

The usual questions of how they'd slept, what they'd prefer in their morning omelets, and if Cinda wouldn't prefer tea over coffee followed. Mr. Cohen strode up the terrace steps after what had obviously been a brisk walk, and Mrs. Cohen rose to inform someone that he'd like his omelet as well.

Cinda tapped the paper. "I couldn't help seeing it. Who glared at you?"

He described the girl again, and Cinda's forehead wrinkled. "I think that was Ruby."

"Smith?"

"They go by Sterling for their cinematic aspirations," she informed him. "Opal was there, too—in iridescent blue. Blonde hair with one of those odd bands about her head—not quite a turban, but…"

"I saw her, too!" Mrs. Cohen exclaimed as she returned. "Very elegant. I pointed her out to Carl."

One by one, they added little things to Gary's list. The crash that hadn't been a gunshot after all. The first smell of smoke. Detective Lindstrom's being shot. Just as he decided he couldn't remember another thing, two things happened. First, Jervis appeared with a girl beside him, both carrying plates in each hand. Then the doorbell rang. Jervis set down plates and disappeared almost without a sound.

They'd taken their first bites when a man in a gray suit stepped onto the terrace. From behind the man, Jervis said, "Mr. Cohen, Detective Arbuckle to see you."

"To see Miss Lucinda Ashton," Arbuckle corrected. He eyed Cinda. "Are you Miss Ashton?"

She nodded. "Yes. How is Detective Lindstrom? We've been concerned."

The detective ignored the question and said, "You'll need to come with me, Miss Ashton."

"Come with you? Why?"

"You're under suspicion for the murders of Edith Flint, Helen Fenwick, Joseph Gorsky, and—"

"Old Joe? Murdered? How?"

Gary rose to protest.

"—and the attempted murder of Detective Lindstrom."

"She didn't do it!" he shouted. "How can you think—?"

Mr. Cohen laid a hand on his arm. "I'll call my lawyer and we'll meet him at the…?"

What they said, Gary didn't hear. He watched as two officers stepped forward and led Lucinda from the table. Mrs. Cohen jumped up to follow, but the detective stopped her. All the while, Gary stood there, numb. *How is this happening?*

The small room they'd taken her to, while dingy, was clean. The detective, Arbuckle, offered her coffee or water and requested a copy of her fingerprints. She'd complied but asked questions about the process. "What do they do, exactly? People talk about them all the time, but I never understood what the point was."

That simple question changed Detective Arbuckle's aloofness to cordiality. He explained the uniqueness of each person's fingerprints, comparing his, a junior officer's, and hers to illustrate. "So, if there is a jewelry store robbery, and a man says he's never been in that store, but his fingerprints are on the case, we know he's lying."

"Fascinating!" she exclaimed. And it was. Who knew just touching something could be so incriminating?

"Don't read many detective novels, do you?"

She shook her head. "I've never acquired the habit, although Gary talks about them sometimes."

The detective leaned back in his chair and produced a cigarette. "I suppose you won't mind, being a cigarillo girl and all?"

Why must men persist in the irrational idea that if I sell the cigarettes, I must not mind the stench of them? Rather than speaking her thoughts aloud, Lucinda merely smiled.

"You do mind." He pocketed the others and left the one he'd meant to smoke on the table. "I suppose a butcher might not enjoy meat after a day of slaughtering the stuff."

"An intriguing way of putting it," she said, unsure what he expected from her.

That seemed to unsettle him. He stared, unblinking, before pulling out a piece of paper from a hidden drawer. What she'd taken for a table must be a writing desk—quite utilitarian, but convenient.

"Your friends," he began, "will be bringing along a lawyer. Do you mind answering a few questions before they arrive, or would you prefer to wait?"

"I have a choice?"

That prompted snickers from both the detective and his officer. "You are not under arrest… yet." He leaned forward, folding his hands on the desk.

Lucinda interrupted him. "Yet?" Perhaps she shouldn't ask, but she couldn't help herself. "What do you mean? Do you intend to arrest me now that I'm here, or only if you find some evidence from your questions that confirms something you suspect?"

Amused, or so it seemed, the man leaned back, crossed his arms over his chest, and eyed her. "I foolishly took you for a rather simple girl."

"But I am."

"You are also an intelligent one. Ignorance of something doesn't preclude intelligence, and I misjudged you."

Realizing he was diverting her from her question, she rephrased it. "May I know what charges you will bring against me, Detective Arbuckle?"

Only then did she hear the ticking of a clock on one wall. A glance at it prompted a second look. She'd seen small table clocks with their little red second hands, but this wall clock looked like one meant for a kitchen, and it too had a second hand that ticked with each motion of the hidden gears. Each tick seemed louder than the last as she waited for a response.

"We have enough evidence to charge you with the murder of Joseph Gorsky. We're comparing fingerprint evidence to determine if we can charge you with the other two murders."

Tears that she hadn't even realized she'd been suppressing rolled down her cheeks. "Poor Joe. He was so kind to me. He even tried to protect me last night when I was late arriving for work." She peered at him through tear-filled eyes. "How'd he die?"

"Come now, Miss Ashton. You could answer that better than we could, don't you think?"

"How? I didn't know—oh, but you think I did. I forgot. You think I killed him, so of course, I'd know how."

A knock preceded an officer poking his head in. "Sir, Mr. Cohen is here with a lawyer for Miss Ashton. Do I show him in?"

"Please."

Only then did Lucinda realize the detective thought her guilty but also had saved the interrogation for when the lawyer arrived. *Can lawyers help the police? I thought they were to protect the accused.*

Everything shifted when a large, round-faced man with bulldog jowls that jiggled with every word spoken entered the room. Questions fired at her one after the other with barely a breath between her answers and his next. In the middle of what the girls at work had called being "Edisoned," her lawyer requested a moment to confer with his "client" before the questioning continued.

"We'll take a ten-minute break. May we offer you more water, Miss Ashton?"

"Please." She offered the detective a smile. "I don't think I'm being very helpful, but I am trying."

The man only offered a returned smile and left. The lawyer turned to her. "From what I make of what he's saying, he thinks you killed Eva Labelle, also known as Edith Flint, and Helen Fenwick out of jealousy over Garrison Prince's attentions to them. He doesn't have the evidence he needs there, but they're working on getting that. I have to ask you. Did you kill these women?"

"No!" Stomach roiling at the recollection of blood and lifelessness, she shuddered and added, "I couldn't have. Besides, anyone in the room would have seen me with a gun and stopped me. Gary would have stopped me. But Detective Arbuckle says he has proof that I killed Joe. I never would have. Never. I couldn't!"

"The evidence there is incriminating. They found a shoe that they believe is yours in the alley—with blood on it. It fits the weapon that likely knocked out this Gorsky fellow."

"May I see the shoe? I could tell them if it was mine."

The lawyer just gaped at her.

NINE

In his third-floor apartment at The Talmage, Gary paced. Mr. Cohen and his lawyer would arrive any minute, surely. *Should have insisted that I go with them.*

Not for the first time, he peered out the window to the street below. Was that Mr. Cohen's car? When a woman showing much too much leg stepped from it, he turned away. Not Mr. Cohen and the lawyer… Somebody or another Darrow, wasn't it?

Gary forced himself to sit in his favorite chair, relax, breathe. As his gaze swept the room, he realized that if he purchased the bungalow in Pasadena—the one he'd been negotiating for a month—he'd have to pack up and move. He'd need crates and boxes, not to mention a moving van. Another glance around him made him reconsider. Would it be a waste to sell the furnishings with the apartment and give the proceeds to Cinda to furnish the Pasadena home?

If she'll have me, he mused.

It hadn't felt dishonest not to talk about his Hollywood persona. After all, he'd introduced himself as he truly was, and he hadn't exactly hidden his acting career. He'd interacted with her at the theater a dozen times or more over the past six months. *But I saw her in the park or at church almost every day. I could have told her.*

His conscience smarted as Gary realized just how evasive and dishonest he'd been. *Lord, please don't allow my sin to affect her.* The words pricked his conscience. He'd been ready to bargain for Cinda's release—total honesty for pardon? "Lousy theology," he muttered.

At the third pass around the room, Gary realized that he'd gotten up again—began pacing. Again. Desperate to do *something*, and determined to prove to Cinda just how serious he was about her, he snatched up the telephone and put a call through to the agent he'd been negotiating with for the house in Pasadena. *She liked it. We'll be happy together there.* For the second time that afternoon, he added to himself, *If she'll have me.*

"Mr. Vance is on the line, Mr. Prinz."

"Hello, Prince. I heard about the goings on over at the Taj. Are you safe? Didn't you have a premiere there last night?"

"I did," he admitted. "And I'm safe enough." *For now. Should have requested the papers. They might say something I don't know.*

"What can I do for you?"

He swallowed hard, hating that the minute he spoke the words, all negotiations would be off. "After showing Cinda around the Oak Knoll place yesterday…" A new thought occurred to him. He'd only shown her the three houses he'd narrowed things down to, and they'd focused on the one he obviously preferred. Perhaps she'd like to see something else available before he just barged in and bought a place for her, no matter how much she'd said she liked it. "I'm thinking we might need to see what else is available before we continue negotiations."

Several long, miserable seconds followed before Vance said, "I am authorized to counter your last offer at just five hundred more. It's a bargain at the listing price, but between you and me, the owner just wants it off his hands."

What? You're giving me ammunition to hold out?

"The fellow had it built for his son, but the boy got pounded badly in the war—shell shock, they call it. Finally did himself in just a couple of weeks back, and now they can't bear to have it anymore."

Oh, the sympathy ploy. To Gary's disgust, it was working, too. "Well, if he'll meet there, perhaps we should take it. Why don't I bring my lawyer over tomorrow, and we'll arrange for the sale?"

His door chimed, and Gary rang off with promises to be at the agent's office at ten o'clock the next morning. *Sure hope Hollister can get away…*

Darrow stood there, taking up most of the doorway as Gary swung open the door to greet them. "Come in. What do we know?"

Mr. Cohen looked around the room before making a beeline for the telephone. "I'll tell Miriam to come now. She'll want to be in on our discussion." Turning away from them, he said, "Yes, operator. I'd like you to put a call in to Musso & Frank Grill…"

Inside a minute, he'd returned to stand behind Gary's sofa. "They'll get her a message and she'll be here in minutes. I'll go meet her downstairs." After a look at Gary, he turned to Darrow. "Wait for me?"

Although it sounded like a question, the order couldn't be mistaken for anything else. The two men sat in the living room making small talk about the stock market, the movie industry, and the new Chrysler Imperial. That one, at least, kept the man's attention.

"Bought myself a Lagonda—pricey but the wife wanted something with a bit of panache." The man released a sigh that could reach the bottom floor and welcome Mrs. Cohen before her husband could hope to enter the elevator. "She's all about appearances now that we're doing well for ourselves. I don't mind telling you that I miss the girl I married."

The man wasn't someone Gary would have usually considered the best source of marriage advice, but how often did a man make a comment like that? "I'm planning to marry soon—I hope, anyway. What advice would you give a man like me—to try to prevent that sort of change, I mean?"

Darrow didn't blink, hesitate, or so much as attempt to couch his words. He blurted out, "Never let your wife know how much you make. She'll spend twice that and wonder why it isn't more."

Not my Cinda…

"And before you think, 'Oh, surely not my precious darling,' recall that I'd have said the same thing twenty years ago. Now I have a wife who can't live without the latest furs, kids who run in the same circles as people who make ten times what I do, and all of them want the luxuries that my income can't provide."

The man looked as if he'd aged ten years just talking about it. "I'm worn out trying to do the impossible for people who don't even appreciate it. I'm living on borrowed money, and my only hope is that my investments will do even better than projected."

"I have investments, but mine are in properties of various sorts. Cinda will know about them, of course, but the idea is for them to provide for us should we find it difficult to make ends meet on a minister's salary."

Darrow leaned forward. "Minister? Aren't you Garrison Prince?"

"I was… right up until midnight. Now I'm only Gary Prinz, Bible scholar."

After plopping back against the sofa, Darrow huffed something incomprehensible and added, "—better make sure that girl of yours knows what she's getting into. Women don't like to learn that their glamorous life is about to become the ladies' aid society, the missionary barrel, and playing organ when the organist has the lumbago."

I'll just be content if she will marry someone who had *that glamorous life at all.*

A knock drove away Gary's thoughts and shifted the awkward discussion to more congenial topics such as how to extract his would-be fiancée from the clutches of the police.

"COME ON, miss. You've got a visitor."

Lucinda rose off the cot provided for her and smoothed the skirt of the blue dress Mrs. Cohen had loaned her and tried not to tug at the way it hung limp about her hips. *Fashion should be the least of my concerns right now.* To the officer, she asked, "Who is the visitor?"

A sly smile followed. "I think you'll be surprised, miss."

Likely Gary, then. He probably thinks this is some publicity thing. "The great movie star shows concern for the woman who murdered his leading lady. Read more on page three."

They didn't take her to the interrogation room again. This time, she sat in a room with three separate tables, all empty now that Gary had risen to greet her. The officer warned against touching. "Sorry, miss. Hands to yourselves, please."

Seated across the scarred table from Gary, Lucinda wondered that she'd never noticed *who* he really was. "You look like the movie posters."

"I've been thinking about that," he murmured, leaning as close as he could. "I shouldn't have left it to you to figure out who I was. I was selfish, Cinda. I cared more about being *me* than I did about being honest and forthright with you. Please say you'll forgive me."

How could she not? She hadn't been forthcoming about her own reasons for coming to Hollywood. "I didn't tell you all of my history, either. I would have," she hastened to add. "Someday…"

"We have time to know the past. My parents gone after the Spanish flu—"

"Mine, too," she added. "I had to quit school—"

Gary would have covered her hands with his if the officer hadn't cleared his throat. "Shh… we'll talk about it later." He shot the officer another look as he murmured, "So the evidence against you…"

"Did you know I have a cellmate?"

Gary frowned. "Is she… safe?"

"I don't know." Lucinda picked at her cuticles as she considered what to say.

Rocking back on the chair legs in a way that would have earned him a sharp rebuke from Mrs. Smith, Gary eyed her. "Are you all right? Did they feed you?" The chair legs clumped back to the floor. "Did you *eat* what they brought you?"

"It was a ham sandwich and an apple. The bread was a bit stale, but the ham was delicious."

Though he said nothing, Lucinda could see the frustration building in him. Gary watched her, his eyes boring into her as if trying to read her thoughts. "Did you arrive late for work yesterday?"

"Yes." She slumped against the back of the chair. "I hope it's warm enough tonight. The cell is a bit chilly, but they said they'd give me a blanket."

"I'll ask."

Lucinda just nodded.

"They found one of your shoes in the alley—or so they say."

"If it had my initials in it…" In her peripheral vision, the officer moved a bit closer. Lucinda rubbed her temple and tried to ignore the awkwardness she'd created.

"It did. But you couldn't have lost your shoe in the alley. You were with someone at all times—"

"I wonder if my rat is hungry."

Again, Gary stared at her, but Lucinda didn't try to meet his gaze. She couldn't. *What must he think of me, being arrested for murder?*

"Cinda…" He shot a look toward the officer before lowering his voice and adding, "Dear…"

She couldn't help but give him a smile.

THAT SMILE WAS NEARLY Gary's undoing. Determination turned into desperation as he focused on getting her out of there. "We must discover what this is all about, but to do that I need your help."

Cinda sat across from Gary, picking at her fingers, almost refusing to meet his gaze much of the time. Each word she spoke held a listless, detached note that tore at his heart. *What have they done to you?*

"I'm sorry, Gary. I need to lie down. I'm so tired. I wish I were back in my own room at Mrs. Smith's."

You want to do what? Back at that place where they locked you in the cellar? Have you gone mad already?

The officer left the room—an obvious breach of some rule to give them a moment of privacy, and Gary didn't waste a second of it. He half dashed around, and half vaulted over the table and pulled Cinda close. "We'll find out what happened, Cinda. We'll get you out—" He'd planned to kiss her in the second it took to reach her, but before he could carry out that scheme, the officer returned.

"I'll go rest now. I hope my cellmate doesn't keep me awake with her chatter."

It's only four o'clock! Why are you so exhausted?

He grabbed his driving gloves and strode from the room, determined to let Mr. Darrow know about her condition. Something had to be terribly wrong. At his car, he hesitated. Home and to the telephone? To the man's office? Find Mr. Cohen?

That thought brought Mrs. Cohen to mind. Perhaps she'd know what they needed to do. She'd bullied Lindstrom into doing what she wanted, so it was possible she'd know how to manage Arbuckle, too.

At the front desk, he requested to use their telephone and in minutes had a dinner invitation at the Cohen home. He headed for the hills, prepared for the teasing he'd endure when they heard how the visit went. *If I could only have stayed, but with her going off like that…*

Headstrong and impulsive. Just like when he was a boy. Hadn't he yet learned to "pause for reflection" as his mother had admonished so often?

The drive back to the Cohen's house gave him plenty of time for reflection. The trouble was, he didn't like what he saw in it. *She didn't affirm or deny that it was her shoe. She just insisted that she could prove if it were. Doesn't she realize that if they think it's hers it's because they have some reason to? How did her shoe get in that alleyway?*

Instead of Jervis meeting him out front, Mrs. Cohen stood there as he pulled up the long, circular drive. The moment he stepped from his car, she began peppering him with questions, all of which were focused on Cinda's wellbeing. "What did she say about the charges?"

"Miriam, maybe he'd like a seat and a drink before he's Edisoned."

The woman actually gaped for a moment before understanding shifted her into hostess mode. "Of course… of course. I'm sorry, Gary. Please come in. I'm sending Jervis to the police station with a hot meal for Lucinda. I've heard the food there isn't much to speak of."

"She said she'd had a sandwich—stale bread but tasty

ham." He groaned. "And that's almost the only thing she really said. I didn't recognize her."

Mr. Cohen pounded his back in what Gary presumed was meant to be a reassuring manner. "She's not had a chance to freshen up all day, my boy…"

Stepping into the large room and seeing Lucinda's empty place on the sofa took the wind out of him. As silly as it felt, he sat next to where she would have been and draped an arm over the back of the couch. "She's listless," he tried to explain. "And what she said made no sense."

"Did you ask her about the shoe?"

"I did, but aside from confirming that she could identify it, there wasn't anything to it. She kept talking about being tired and her 'cellmate' and how she wanted to go back to Mrs. Smith's, which made no sense. Yesterday she insisted she couldn't go back."

The Cohens exchanged looks, but at least neither of them told him he'd lost his mind. He hung his head in his hands. "I think she's given up, and who can blame her? Accused of murder when she can't possibly have done it, locked up in a rat-infested jail. It's enough to discourage anyone."

"We'll go back to the theater tonight," Mr. Cohen said. "We'll take flashlights, and we'll scour the whole area for *something* that points to anyone but Lucinda. She didn't do it, so we just have to prove it."

"*They* should have to prove she did." Gary jumped to his feet and paced. "But they think they have proven it with those shoes. She *couldn't* have. She was with us the whole time!"

A slight clearing of her throat brought both men's attentions to Miriam Cohen. "Actually, there were just a few short minutes where she dashed back—just before the lights went out, do you remember? If the police find out about that…"

Once more, Gary sank back onto the sofa, and once more he buried his face in his hands. "What are we going to do?"

TEN

Lying on one side, Lucinda couldn't help but feel like a modern-day Ezekiel. *Although he was a prophet… and not a woman.* With that distinction firmly rooted in her mind, she lay there, watching the small hole she'd decided belonged to a mouse. The slightly rounded sides and pointed top made it look like the windows and archways of the theater, which only filled her with despair.

He might come out… if he's in there. It would be the most interesting thing to happen all day. That felt disloyal to Gary, but *his* visit hadn't been as satisfactory as she'd hoped.

A door opened at the end of the long hallway. Footsteps beat a steady rhythm that grew louder with each passing second. The jingle of keys. Lucinda sat up. *Must be dinnertime.*

"You've got nice friends, Miss Ashton. They've sent you dinner—hot, too."

"Dinner? Really? Can they do that?"

The man swung open the door and carried in a basket with an enamel lunch box and two thermoses. "We had to inspect it all, of course." He gave her a cheeky grin. "Can't have you filing your way out of here or anything."

While her insides screamed, *I'd never!* Lucinda just smiled. "Thank you ever so much."

"Cheer up, miss. They're not likely to hang you—almost always commute a woman's sentence."

This time, Lucinda really looked at the man. His bald head made his forehead look never ending. Bushy eyebrows with wiry hairs jutting out at odd angles. A slightly crooked tie. Chipped front tooth. "I didn't kill anyone," she said, more to remind herself of that fact than anything. "They can hang me if they want, but it won't make me guilty."

After a look and then another, the officer shrugged and left the cell, locking it behind him. "Just let me know when you're done with those. I'll wash 'em up for you to give to your feller when he comes back."

My "feller" has better things to do than sit around and commiserate with me… I hope.

Lucinda had tried praying all afternoon and had failed. This time her prayers poured out but made no sense, even to her. *Didn't Gary say something about the Holy Spirit making our prayers acceptable? Does He make them comprehensible, too?* The question mocked her as soon as her mind caught up to it. *As if God doesn't know what I want to say. If He didn't, He wouldn't be worth serving.*

Roast beef and gravy poured out of the thermos. She'd never imagined poking beef into a container like that, but it worked, and the little plate in the lunch box was just the right size to hold it. A small jar held peas and onions—just a degree or two above lukewarm but still delicious. The other thermos held lemonade. Wrapped in waxed paper, she found a couple of buttered rolls and a piece of cake. It was a dinner fit for a king—or queen, rather—as far as she was concerned.

Before she'd eaten her cake and finished her lemonade, the door opened at the end of the hall. Another pair of shoes walked down, but these sounded different to her. When a man appeared at the door in a dark gray suit and black tie, she nodded. "Detective Arbuckle. Have you arrested the real murderer?"

"We think so."

Her relief was short lived. "Oh… you think that's me." Lucinda rewrapped her cake in the waxed paper and put it back in the lunch box. "What can I do for you?"

"We'd like to ask a few more questions."

I'd like to ask to leave, but I'm not likely to receive a favorable response.

The keys jangled and the cell door swung open. "This way, if you please."

What if I don't please? Lucinda couldn't help but smile at herself. *Feeling a bit saucy, aren't you?*

She caught the man looking at her and turned that smile on him. "I don't recall anything more, but it is nice to have a bit of a walk…"

All along the bland hallway, to the next, and only slightly less bland hallway, and into the equally bland interrogation room with its plain table and uncomfortable chairs, Lucinda's mind raced. *Did Gary find something already? Is that why he has more questions?*

"Have a seat, Miss Ashton."

She sighed. "Must I? Standing feels good. I don't know why I didn't think to pace about my cell."

"You'll have plenty of time for that, later. I'm afraid I must insist. I would also appreciate if you would remove your right shoe."

"My—?"

Perhaps it was the unexpectedness of the question, but Lucinda found herself complying. She offered it to him, and he set it on the table. Silence reigned.

Arbuckle shifted his attention between the shoe, Lucinda, and back to the shoe again. Perspiration beaded along Lucinda's hairline and in other, more uncomfortable places. The part of her that wanted to break down into tears and beg him to let her go warred with a part of her that heretofore she'd not known existed. That part ached to lean forward and whisper, "Do you want to know how I did it?"

Oh, how she could imagine the look on his face when he said yes, and she said, "So do I."

However, antagonizing a detective was likely a poor way to encourage the police to release her for lack of evidence or whatever they called it. Instead, she waited yet again. An officer appeared with a glass of water for her.

"Thank you."

"I have a question for you, Miss Ashton."

"So you said." A flash of irritation on his face prompted her to add, "What question was that?"

He tapped the shoe. "If a dozen of these were lined up across the desk here—twelve identical-looking shoes, would you be able to identify yours?"

"Yes, I think so. See I—"

"Don't tell me how yet. Let me guess."

A knot formed in her stomach. *It has to be my shoe. But how?*

"I see you realize I must know how you've marked them."

"I do." She leaned forward and added, "What I don't understand is how I could have left a shoe in the alley when I left the building by the front side door with both of my shoes on my feet."

THEY SAT at a card table in a billiard room that held several card tables, the obligatory billiard table, and a couple of wing-backed chairs. Gary had been impressed for the minute or so he'd been distracted from their purpose, but now his focus remained on their plan. First, they'd recreate the previous evening and then they'd go see the Taj Mahal Theater for themselves.

Mr. Cohen, who had become simply "Albert" after a day

of interaction, pulled out the *Los Angeles Times, Examiner, Express,* and *Herald* newspapers. He passed each of them a pad of paper, a pencil, and one of the newspapers. "Write down anything of significance that you can find about the fire, Lucinda's arrest, or either of those detectives. If there are witness names, we need that, too."

Although she picked up her pencil and pulled the paper close, Miriam gazed at her husband as if contemplating something. "Did Harold suggest this?"

Without looking up, the man began writing at the top of his pad. "Yes. He's having his men look into it, too, but it helps having someone who was there go over it as well. They'll question us tomorrow."

"Ugh. The police interrogation was enough," she said. "The questions alone made me doubt my own innocence."

Gary's newspaper was the *Los Angeles Express*. The headline punched him in the gut. CIGARILLO GIRL ARRESTED FOR MURDERS AT TAJ MAHAL. He kept reading. *In a twist of irony, the beloved Eva Labelle's last gasp may have been the work of one of the theater's cigarillo girls, the very one who sold Hollywood royalty, Garrison Prince, the star's last package of "gaspers."*

"This is brutal."

"So is mine." Miriam pulled the leftover paper toward her and read the headline aloud. "'Jealousy Cited as Motive for Murder.'" She gave the paper an impatient shake and continued reading. "'According to people intimately connected with her, Miss Lucinda Ashton came to Hollywood with cinematic aspirations but only found work as a cigarillo girl at the Taj Mahal Theater. While her employer and supervisor had only high praise for her work ethic, others who knew her say she was of a jealous and vindictive temperament when faced with the success of the starlets who left her out of the cinema limelight—'"

"That isn't true! I don't know that Lucinda ever wanted to have anything to do with pictures."

The Cohens exchanged glances—amused ones? He couldn't be sure, but it certainly looked like it. Miriam reached over and squeezed his hand. "There is usually some truth behind these stories. I suspect a sweet girl like Lucinda enjoyed putting on skits and plays with her playfellows back home—where is that, again?"

"She's from Oregon."

"There, you see. Probably a small-town girl with no idea of the cattiness and pettiness in the industry. I suspect she arrived, saw what starlets were like, and decided to save up to go back home or set herself up somewhere else."

There was some truth to it. They'd talked enough about their pasts for him to know she had no future in Oregon, so she'd come to California to better her life. "She's saving to take a secretarial course," he insisted. "She never mentioned an interest in pictures."

This time, Albert stepped in. "A sweet girl like her isn't going to risk confessing something like that to a future clergyman, especially one she admires. It's likely that she'd changed her mind as Miriam suggested and chose not to share that part of her plans until she knew you well enough to trust you."

And now you've ensured she doesn't—trust you, that is. Despite that discouraging thought, Gary couldn't help his hopes rising at the idea she kept it from him because she admired him. *How can I know someone so well and so little at the same time? Can you marry someone you don't know fully?*

Determined not to be sidetracked from his purpose, Gary scribbled down a few names from the article. That got him thinking about other names—names of those who had been in the theater. He wrote down everyone he could remember and a description of those he saw but didn't know.

The task took longer than he'd expected. There were the headlines, of course, but Albert had them read every word of the papers to see if anything was mentioned in any other article. Gary's refusal to sign on for another six years with Imperial still commandeered interest in other sections—society, financial, and even an editorial on the unreasonable expectations of the Hollywood elite. *Actors such as Garrison Prince make more money in a week than the average household earns in a year. Will the American people continue to support such excesses in their unquenchable thirst for exciting entertainment?*

"Brutal."

"What now?" Miriam rose and leaned over his shoulder to read. "People like that with their moralistic high ground and no concept of the public's fickle attention. Of course, we must pay a premium for good talent. We work them long, hard hours without breaks and perhaps for three or four years. Then, unprepared for a vocation, we send them off to survive and hope they saved enough to get by on."

It had been his thought as well, but hearing her defend Hollywood's business model left a bitter taste in his mouth. *Just as well that I got out when I did. I was learning to like the luxuries that I can't hope to afford later.*

"Done with that one, Gary?" Albert pushed his across and reached for the *Express*. "Go over mine, will you? We need to be sure we miss nothing."

The *Los Angeles Times* headline would have coldcocked him if it had a fist. THREE DEAD AFTER MURDEROUS RAMPAGE AT THEATER.

ELEVEN

Albert's chauffeur let them off behind the theater and inched the car out of sight, promising to meet them at the diner in an hour. Flashlights in hand, they made their way to the alleyway that led to the building's back entrance. The stench of charred, soaked wood lingered in the air. He kicked at a blackened something and a puff of soot sent him choking. That's when he realized something. "Why isn't this cordoned off?"

Miriam shrugged and picked her way around debris. "Don't know. I thought we'd be avoiding police on guard, but there's nothing."

"I suppose they don't expect people sneaking around a half-burned building on a Saturday night," Albert said.

Movement to his right made Gary jump and Charleston his way away from the source. Two glowing eyes met his as a mangy cat emerged from beneath a small pile of rubble. With a yowl, the cat darted across his path and out of sight.

Gary could only hope he'd managed to hide the skittish move on his part. Albert's chuckle hinted that it wasn't likely. "I keep expecting someone to step out and say, 'Stop in the name of the law!'"

"Do they actually say that?" As she asked, Miriam kicked over that pile of rubble the cat had lurked under. "And where do you think the back door was?"

Gary pointed to where a frame sat cockeyed and charred. "There, I'd say. Why?"

But the woman didn't answer, exactly. She moved to where that door had been and swept the area with her flashlight. "I wonder where they found that shoe?"

"The detective told Darrow and Miss Ashton that it was in the alley."

With the flashlight shining into the charred, unstable walls, Miriam mused, "How…?" She whirled to face Gary, and the flashlight nearly blinded him. "How long was she gone when she followed that girl back here?"

"Ummm…"

"Long enough to get through whatever you have to go through to go all the way out here and into the alley, lose a shoe, find another one when she got back in the building, and get back to us?"

Hope welled in him, hope he hadn't realized he'd begun to lose. "No. Not even if she'd been gone twice as long for sure."

"And she arrived at our house with both shoes?"

That question prompted a new idea. "Even if she hadn't, we'd have been with her when she lost it, wouldn't we? Doesn't that prove she didn't then? We'd have *known*?"

Albert insisted it proved only that she hadn't lost it before they all left. "But if there wasn't time to get out here, lose a shoe, find another one, and get back, that is significant."

Before Gary could ask what they should do with that information, a voice called out and the wide beam of a large flashlight blinded him for the second time that night. "Theo?" The fellow stepped closer. "Oh, no. What are you doing here?"

Although Gary would have answered, Albert Cohen stepped up. "We were here last night—left through the side door. Lost a cuff link. We're looking for it. What are *you* doing here?"

To cover his protest, Gary coughed. The man who had started to identify himself as a theater employee turned his attention on Gary. "Mr. Prince?"

"Yes?"

"You know this fella?"

"I met him last night in the melee."

The man swung his flashlight to Albert, over to Miriam, and back to Gary. "Did he lose a cuff link?"

"Don't know," Gary said. "I'm just along to look around. If I find one, I'm sure it'll be his."

"Probably be ruined," the fellow remarked. "Still, you'd better come back tomorrow. In the daylight. You can see better and the manager's around." His voice lowered, "Not that I don't like to hear someone tryin' to help Miss Ashton, but I've got my job to worry about. The wife is worried enough about me gettin' let go now that the theater's closed."

Smart chap. Nicely done.

As if he hadn't been put in his place, Albert Cohen stuck out his hand. "We found something that should help. Thank you for your understanding."

"Of course," the man said. He didn't, however, take the proffered hand. "Just come around in the morning. Or call the manager. Meanwhile, I'll keep my eye open for…" After a meaningful pause he added, "That *cuff link.*"

Without anything else they could do, the Cohens and Gary took off for the all-night diner on Franklin. For coffee, pie, and time to decide what to do next.

SUNDAY MORNING, Lucinda awoke with the distressing realization that she wouldn't have dinner with Gary. He wouldn't ask her to marry him today. And if something didn't change quickly, she might never marry at all. *Why did I ever come to this wretched town?*

The moment the question formed itself, she answered it. *Because I needed out of Wooten before I became a true indentured servant. Do those still exist?*

She rose and called for the guard to take her to the lavatory. In there, she washed as best she could and tried to smooth her rumpled dress. The delicate fabric hadn't worn well, not having been designed as jail garb. *I'm a criminal,* Lucinda mused. *In the eyes of the law, anyway, I'm a criminal.*

Before that thought could send her heart spiraling down into a well of despair, she turned her attention to the rat's nest her hair had become during the night. Though she didn't hold much hope for getting it arranged fashionably, Lucinda unpinned what still hung in place, finger-combed what she could, braided it, and pinned it all at the nape of her neck. *I probably look like a spinster now.*

The guard waited for her outside the door, and a look of appreciation told her she'd managed to make herself look at least a little presentable. He must have realized Lucinda noticed, because he said, "Sorry, miss. Most ladies hardly wash their hands and faces. It's like they think the more pathetic they look the more lenient the judge will be, but it just don't work that way."

"I imagine," Lucinda said as she approached her cell again, "that judges have to look at facts rather than faces."

"Just so, miss. Just so. Still, it'll be a nice change for Judge Whittier to have a pretty face that don't look like it's just escaped a cat fight, if you'll pardon my sayin'." As he pulled the door shut, he gave her a weak smile. "Tomorrow'll be here before you know it. I can't say for sure, of course, but I 'spect they'll give you a hefty bail. Hope you've got someone to put it up for you."

There was a question in his statement, but Lucinda lost track of it somewhere. She sank back onto the cot and stared at his shiny shoes. *Bail. I'll need bail. I don't even have a hundred dollars saved. That probably isn't enough. They'll want thousands.*

Only when the clunk of shoes on the floor broke into her thoughts did Lucinda realize the shiny shoes had disappeared. A sweep of the cell prompted her to fluff the pillow and fold her blanket. She didn't like sitting on the single sheet they'd used to cover the mattress, so she spread it out again and stood back to survey the results. Drab brownish-gray against the white walls and gray floor did nothing to make the room appealing. Even her skirt looked dull and uninteresting next to the blanket.

The rat-a-tat of his shoes returning told her something was up. The officer grinned at her. "You've got company, miss. She brought food and talked the desk sergeant into letting you eat it while she talks to you."

"She? Mrs. Smith?"

The man screwed up his face and shook his head. "No… that wasn't the name. One of them Jewish names—rich lady. I can tell you that."

"Mrs. Cohen, I expect."

"That's her. She's waitin' in the visitor's room. Come with me."

Despite the mutters, orders, and grunts of the officer on guard, Mrs. Cohen hugged Lucinda the moment she entered the room. "Are you well? Are they treating you properly? We'll file a complaint—"

"Everyone is being as kind as is reasonable," Lucinda assured her.

"Then sit and eat while I tell you what we found out."

Sitting, but ignoring the order to eat, Lucinda shot a look at their guard before asking, "Will Gary be coming today?"

"I think so." Mrs. Cohen sat across from her and made a pointed stare at the untouched breakfast before adding, "And he'll be there in the morning at the bail hearing."

"I don't want him there for that." It felt peevish, but the

idea of Garrison Prince sitting there, listening as they announced a bail he could pay without noticing and she couldn't hope to afford, hurt her pride more than she was prepared to suffer. "Please tell him I'd love for him to visit afterward, but—"

There, Mrs. Cohen broke in. She ignored the rules and reached across to pat Lucinda's hand. The guard protested. "Oh, go away with you. This girl needs comfort, and your matron already examined my pockets and handbag. What more do you want from me?"

"Rules—"

"Are designed to prevent illegal smuggling of contraband and such like. I'm simply comforting a young woman who went through a harrowing ordeal on Friday night—something it seems you all have forgotten."

"Guilty of—" the man continued.

Mrs. Cohen would have none of that. "Nothing, and in the eyes of the law, until she's *proven* guilty, she is innocent. Now let us be."

"Can't do that. It's my job—"

What else they said, Lucinda didn't hear. Her ears buzzed and her brain burned. She pulled the plate toward her and ate without tasting a bite. Only Mrs. Cohen's sharp, "Lu*cinda*!" pulled her from her befuddled state.

"Yes?"

"I asked if you remembered where you went when you went into the back. You weren't gone all that long, and—"

Squeezed from all sides even with nothing touching her, Lucinda gasped at the pain and compressed lungs. "I wish I was home in my own bed."

Mrs. Cohen stopped mid-sentence and gaped at her. "You —?" She blinked and shook her head. "You said you wanted to go back there only to get your things. That Mrs.—"

"I want my things. A change of clothes and my parents' picture. I want my hairbrush and the Bible Gary bought me."

Once she started talking, Lucinda found it impossible to stop. "I need to find my shoes and return my uniform to the theater." Her mind argued that, so she chattered there, too. "Except they have nowhere to store them now, I suppose. I wonder if I'll be charged for it." With a forkful of eggs halfway to her mouth, Lucinda froze, blinked at the obviously confused Mrs. Cohen and asked, "Do you think I'll be paid for Friday night?"

Ignoring that question, Mrs. Cohen focused on one statement. "Find your—?"

"Did I tell you I finally saw my cellmate? He's not really afraid of me, but he does watch me a lot—curious little fellow…"

"They have a man—"

"Not a man," Lucinda argued. She leaned forward and whispered, "A rat."

The Reverend Jack Clark preached at The Church of the Open Door of Los Angeles that Sunday morning, something about Jesus' devotion to prayer and fasting and knowing the Scriptures well enough to refute Satan's lies. That much Gary heard and took to heart. What else the man said, he didn't know. Gary was lost in questions, suppositions, theories, and other vagaries of the past few days.

I hope Mrs. Cohen discovers just how long Lucinda was in the back. At the time it seemed like hours, but looking back, it couldn't have been more than a minute or two. With people back there and such, how could she find her *shoe, carry it with her out the back door, down to the alley, and then return without it? Makes no sense.*

"'Seek ye *first*,' Jesus said. Then He told us what the result would be. In II Chronicles 7:14, we're told, 'If my people, which are called by my name, shall humble themselves, and pray, and seek my face, and turn from their wicked ways; then will I hear from heaven, and will forgive their sin, and will heal their land.' Again," the preacher insisted. "We're given an order of events. We obey and *then* the Lord blesses those efforts."

Does that work for proving a young lady innocent? If we… pray, He'll… what? Write the name of the murderer on a wall? It sounds like a dime novel.

A moment later, despite being what he'd known all along, Gary's hopes plummeted. "This isn't a cause and effect," Reverend Clark insisted. "This is a generality. As Jesus reminded us in Matthew 5:45, 'for he maketh his sun to rise on the evil and on the good, and sendeth rain on the just and on the unjust.' However, it behooves us to obey His commands just as children ought to obey their parents. And God, like any good Father, enjoys bestowing gifts and blessings on His beloved children."

And what do Your children do when the "rulers" of this world falsely imprison them? How do we appeal to You and receive favor? How do we know what steps to take?

He couldn't prove Lucinda innocent. She'd left them long enough to do someone harm if not long enough to lose a shoe. But anyone could have had those shoes in hand as they rushed out of the burning building. Why would she have two pair of shoes? He didn't know. What possible motive would she have for killing someone she spoke of with such fondness? Did police use the detective novel formula of means, motive, and opportunity to ferret out their suspects? Did having only one of those—possibly two—count enough against her to have her arrested? How had that happened?

Those questions repeated themselves even as he stepped out into the rain without opening his umbrella. By the time he reached his car, Gary knew two things. First, he must speak to Lucinda immediately. Second, he was soaked.

TWELVE

The new deli on Sunset Boulevard, Greenblatt's, teemed with diners eager for a good meal. Gary waited with more impatience than he'd admit to, but he was determined to bring something tasty to Lucinda—to make a picnic lunch for her right there in the visiting room. *One more day. We'll pay her bail, get her out, and find out who did this thing. There can't be enough evidence to convict. Perhaps the judge will just let her go.*

"What can I get for you?"

Gary jerked his head up to the menu board and read off a couple of things without really considering what he asked for. "And a couple of bottles of Coke, please."

Juggling the paper bag with sandwiches in one hand and the Coke bottles in the other, Gary made his way out of the deli and to the curb where his Studebaker waited. *I should be practicing my proposal for our dinner this evening, not taking a picnic lunch to a jail house.*

He'd meant for tonight to be the first time he picked her up at her boarding house—like a gentleman should. *As a lady deserves. I want her to feel respected, Lord. Right now, she probably feels like a criminal even while knowing she isn't.*

One bottle of Coke began to slip when he opened the door, so Gary flung himself into the car and allowed the bottle to land on the seat. "Whew!" That sigh of relief faded as he saw the smashed bag. "Ugh."

Gary pulled away from the curb, a car's horn blaring and hinting he might have pulled out too soon, but he consoled himself with the idea that even smashed sandwiches were probably better than dry bread and lukewarm milk. Cinda hadn't *said* the milk was lukewarm, but he couldn't imagine dry bread on sandwiches with *cold* milk.

The romances a cousin had devoured would have described the continual drizzle as, "The day wept for the forlorn Cinda, trapped in a stone …" Something or other. Dungeon? Crypt of dashed hopes? Oh, definitely that one. Gary knew it because that cousin had taken weeks to read a single book due to her propensity to pause at every paragraph of purple prose and gush over it to anyone near enough for her to pounce on.

Mrs. Cohen rose from a chair near the door when he arrived. "I've been waiting," she whispered.

"Why are you whispering?" His "Why" had been spoken in a normal tone, but at the glare she'd given him, he'd swallowed the rest into a choked murmur.

"I don't know." He could almost hear her insisting that she knew it made no sense, but she had to do it anyway. "Ask her about why she wants to go home. Ask about her cellmate."

That struck him as odd, considering those were the only two things she'd mentioned to him. "Why—?"

An officer came forward, ready to greet them. Mrs. Cohen squeezed his arm and told him to call when he was done. "I'll go with you to her rooming house. Get her to give you a note allowing you to take her things."

While the officer in charge went to bring in Cinda, Gary spread out a small tablecloth he'd brought from home. The round edges looked odd on the slightly rectangular table, but the sandwiches looked better on it, anyway. The Cokes—oh, he'd forgotten her flowers in the car!

Gary dashed out the door and down the hall. The man at the desk asked what was wrong, and Gary told about the flowers. "There's nothing to put them in. She can't have a vase, man."

"A tin can? If I can find one? Even still, just on the table while we eat would be all right, wouldn't it?"

Not for the first time since he'd become a household name, Gary found someone making an exception for him, and he had no doubt it was to tell his wife that Garrison Prince had been in *his* station that day. That the man had helped *the* Garrison Prince create a romantic lunch in their visitation room. *And for the first time ever, I'm grateful for that—truly grateful.*

Cinda was just reaching for the chair when Gary arrived back to their picnic. He ignored the scowling policeman and gave her the flowers, hugged her, kissed her temple, and held her chair. "We're going to pretend it's not raining outside and that we're in the park on *our* bench, having a picnic like we've done so many times."

As he reached for his sandwich, she cocked her head in that way she only did when he'd confused her. "Are you going to pray? You always pray at our little picnics."

What else could he do but pray? Although he kept his petition short and mostly to the point, he couldn't help but raise his voice just a bit and say, "And Lord, show these men the folly of their focus on Cinda so that the true murderer can be caught before he manages to escape."

As he raised his head, Gary saw Cinda's still bowed. Several seconds passed before he noticed the whiteness of her folded hands. When her gaze finally met his again, tears brimmed in her eyes. "I want to go home."

"You can't, Cinda. Not there. Mrs. Cohen—"

She brushed the tears from her eyes and picked up the sandwich. "I *must* go home, Gary. It's imperative."

As he rushed out the door and down the steps to the soggy street, Gary shot a glare back at the building that housed his… well, she *should* be his fiancée by now. A glance at his wristwatch amended that thought. *Or nearly so, anyway.*

The anger he'd managed to suppress as Cinda insisted she did *not* want him at the bail hearing the next morning boiled over at the sight of a boy running one hand over the hood of his Studebaker. "Get your hands off that!"

A small head shot up. Two great, nearly black eyes met his gaze even in the rain, and the boy backed away. "Sor—"

"Hey…"

The kid turned to go, but Gary caught his arm. "I'm sorry. I had no right to shout at you like that."

Those wide eyes looked suspiciously watery, but considering the raindrops that dripped off the boy's nose, it might not have been Gary's bark. He gave a weak smile. "It's a spiffy car, mister. The cat's pajamas!"

Getting wetter by the second, despite the slowed drizzle, Gary still stood there, smiling. "Where's your hat?"

"Ain't got one."

"You don't, huh?"

The kid shook his head. "Nossir." Then he took a step closer and cocked his head. "Hey… ain't you…?" Another shake. "Naw…"

Gary stuck out a hand to shake the boy's and said, "Gary Prinz."

"Ga—well, you *are,* him, ain'tcha?" As if he'd just noticed the hand, the boy pumped it a couple of times, grinning all the while. "Wow. Shakin' the hand of the guy what's in all the pitchers."

Does your mother correct your speech all the time like mine did? Would she tell you not to say "ain't" and remind you to enunciate so others can discern whether you're speaking of vessels or cinematographic images?

"And your name?"

"Herbie, sir. Herbie Grant."

The name… how many times had Cinda spoken of a boy she felt certain was an orphan living alone on the streets. *"His name is Herbert, and he's the darlingest boy. I always find errands for him to help him earn a bit of money. I don't know how he survives, because I've given him the chance to steal from me a dozen times, and he never does."*

"I think you know a friend of mine." Gary opened the door. "Cinda Ashton."

"Oh, Miss Cindy's the best." As if someone had jerked a light chain, the boy's entire demeanor lit up. "Oh! *You're* her Gary?"

Her Gary. I like the sound of that. Gary just nodded.

"Wow. She never told me you were *Garrison Prince*!"

"I don't think she realized." He gestured to the car. "Want a ride? I'm going to meet friends over at Cinda's place and see if we can get her things out of her room."

Even as the boy climbed in, he asked, "She's leavin'?"

Gary thought he heard a tremble in the lad's tone. As he climbed in behind the wheel, he answered. "Yes. She had a bad experience there on Friday, and she doesn't want to go back."

"Well, I don't blame her. That Ruby Smith is a nasty bit of a thing. She might look like Miz Pickford, but she sure ain't as sweet."

And how do you know anything about how sweet Mary Pickford is or isn't?

"Leastways, the time I saw her outside Grauman's she was." With a jerk, the boy grabbed the door handle. "Hey, how come you's gettin' Miss Cindy's stuff? Why ain't she doin' it?"

A lump grew in his throat, choking him as he pointed to the station doors. "She's locked up in there until tomorrow."

"What for? Miss Cindy ain't never done nothin' wrong!"

Lord, may I take him home, feed him, give him some decent clothes, and a start on a new vocabulary?

"They think she did, but they don't have any real proof. Tomorrow, we'll pay her bail, and her lawyer will go to work proving she's innocent."

"Naw, that ain't how it works, mister. The other guy—the police lawyer. He's the one what has ta prove she done it. I knows, cause I listens when they let me in."

Or, rather, when they don't see you sneak in, I suspect.

Driving by Cinda's boarding house, Gary saw the Cohens hadn't arrived yet. "I'm waiting for friends to help pack her things, and they aren't here yet." He pulled over beneath a jacaranda that dripped with water and blossoms. Turning to Herbie, Gary asked, "Would you like a ride home?"

The boy's eyes narrowed. "What're ya playin' at, Mr. Prince? If you know Miss Cindy—"

"And I do."

Reaching for the door handle, Herbie said, "What color's her new dress?"

"Green, brown, and yellow. Just like her eyes."

"Where'd she live before here?"

Instead of pointing out that he obviously knew where the young lady lived, Gary answered the question. "Oregon—small town in the middle."

"Middleton."

Gary shook his head. "No, that's up in the northwestern corner."

A grin spread across Herbie's face. "Yeah. Don't make much sense to me. Middleton should be in the middle." A moment later, a chuckle began. "Ya got me. Plumb forgot what I was sayin'. Cinda knows I ain't got a ma anymore. She don't say it, but she knows. How come she didn't tell ya?"

"She did. I was just confirming her suspicion." Gary gazed out through the rain speckled windshield. "Where will you sleep tonight?"

It took several seconds, but Herbie's quiet response finally reached Gary. "There's a church over on Sunset—the Blessed Somethin' or 'nother."

"Sacrament."

"Right. Well, it's open all night, and I sleeps there most days. The Father guy, he lets me take a bath sometimes. Gives me a good meal, too. I go to the mess sometimes, but my ma was a Baptist, see, so I cain't be a Cath'lic. Wouldn't be right."

Only by the grace of God did Gary not snicker. *The mess. I've got to remember to tell Cinda that one.* He had to say something, though. "Didn't anyone tell you there are places that'll take you in—"

"Ain't goin' to no orph'nage. Ma lived in one of them places, and she telled me when she was dyin', she said, 'Herbie, don't you let them put you in an orph'nage. If they come for ya, you go nice and quiet like you're pleased for th' help. Then, when they puts ya to bed, ya sneak out and run. Trust me. They's bad places'."

The Cohen's car came toward them at that moment. Gary pointed. "That's who I'm waiting for."

Herbie started to climb out, but Gary stopped him. "Look. I can't make you go somewhere else. I won't even try. But if you want to come home with me, you're welcome to sit here until I'm done."

"Why? What's a fella like you want with a kid like me hangin' 'round?"

This time, Gary couldn't hide a grin. "Well, mostly because I like you, Herbie. However, even if I didn't, Cinda loves you and would want me to try to help if I could. And I can." He pushed open his door, and when he turned back, Gary felt sure the kid would be gone before he returned. On impulse, he pulled off his hat. “Here. It’s too big, but you need something to keep the rain off your face.”

Though Herbie took it, he just gazed at Gary, unspeaking.

“See you around, kid.”

With that, he strode off across the street, certain he’d never see the boy again.

THIRTEEN

Somewhere deep in the house, a phonograph record played "Tiger Rag" as Gary knocked on the screen door. Behind him, the Cohens whispered—something about the place looking more respectable than they'd expected. The words rankled, as if casting aspersions on Lucinda's character.

He must have stiffened or showed some other reaction, because Albert murmured, "After locking that girl in the cellar, we didn't know what to expect of these people."

Even Gary couldn't argue against that, as much as he might wish to. Still, a girl clattering down the stairs to answer his eventual twist of the old-fashioned doorbell interrupted any response he might have made. "Oh, hello. I thought you might be—" Her face fell. "But I see you aren't." Three seconds later as she stepped up to the door and saw just who stood there, that same expression changed again. "Oh!"

Gary pulled out the note Cinda had written out for him to give to Mrs. Smith—the one allowing him and the Cohens to remove her belongings from the premises. "I'm here to retrieve Lucinda Ashton's things. Miss…"

"Anderson. Mrs. Smith—"

"Will resume this interview, Patty. Thank you for coming to answer the bell, but I can manage from here."

The woman who stood before him wore a crisp apron over what must be a Sunday dress. Her hair, shoes, and even the tasteful pearls around her neck bespoke modest gentility. "How may I help you…" Her forehead furrowed. "Pardon me, but you bear a striking resemblance to…" She swallowed and opened the door. "Forgive me. Come in, please."

They followed the woman into the house and into a small, tastefully arranged parlor. "Please have a seat, Mr.…"

Gary held out his hand. "My name is Gary Prinz. This is Mr. and Mrs. Albert Cohen."

"Albert *Cohen*! Where have I heard that name before?"

He might have answered if not for the fact that her features held no hint of confusion. It felt off, somehow, but Gary couldn't decide what about it didn't ring true.

Gary was spared the awkwardness of an introduction by Albert thrusting out his hand and saying, "Albert Cohen, Sunset Studios."

"Oh, *that Albert Cohen!*" Again, her words held something strange in their emphasis. "Please do be seated. How may I help you?"

He'd almost lowered himself into a chair opposite the woman when he recalled the letter. Wavering for a moment as he tried to reverse the trajectory of his backside, Gary passed it to her. "I'm here on behalf of Lucinda Ashton. She requests that we gather her personal belongings from her room and take them with us. We understand there's also the matter of the rest of the month's rent."

Without a word, the woman sat, ankles together, knees to one side, back ramrod straight. It seemed as if, after a quick scan of the contents, the woman reread each word with particular care—excessive care, in his opinion. Once finished and presumably satisfied, she refolded the letter and passed it back to him. "I apologize for your inconvenience, but I cannot release personal belongings to anyone but Miss Ashton. It isn't done."

The languid timbre of the woman's tone belied the cunning in her fixed gaze—fixed on Albert rather than Gary. He held it in his hands and watched her for a moment before saying, "Pardon me, but you have no right to possessions which are not yours."

A slow smile formed as Mrs. Smith swung her gaze to him. "One might say the same of a disgraced actor, mightn't one?"

With a *bang!* that rang through the house, another girl allowed the screen door to snap shut behind her and charged into the room. "Mother! The papers are full of Cinder's capers! Isn't it a scream!" At that moment, she saw Gary sitting there beside her mother and gave a real one. "You—You're *Garrison Prince!*"

Both men had risen, and out of courtesy he didn't feel, Gary offered his hand. "Miss Smith?"

"Sterling—my screen name. Smith is too, too staid, don't you think?" She linked an arm through his. "Now, tell me what you're doing at my house! Opal will be so jealous to hear she missed you for her old fuddy-duddy lessons."

Lessons on a Sunday?

"Ruby, dear, our guests are here for Lucinda's things. I informed them that, of course, I cannot hand over private property to anyone, even someone of Mr. Prince's former station." Despite the gentle tones and "dear," the edge on Mrs. Smith's voice might have sliced through Cinda's cell bars without a catch.

"Oh, who cares about her old stuff. It's all out of date, anyway. She doesn't have much—just that old suitcase and a few small crates—"

Mrs. Smith rose. "Ruby, would you please see if we have enough cookies to go with coffee?"

"What? *Me*? I've got a—"

Albert interrupted. "Did you say your name was Ruby Sterling?"

The girl turned to him, her pouty red lips twisted into a sneer. "Who's asking?"

He rose and held out his hand. "Albert Cohen, Miss Sterling. I've heard of you and your sister."

The effort it took for Gary *not* to snicker proved harder than not sneezing after inhaling spilled pepper. Ruby's jaw slackened. "Wow! You're the big cheeses of Sunset Studios!"

"Ruby, really!" For the first time, Mrs. Smith's reaction looked and sounded genuine.

"Mother, we've tried for *months* to get auditions at Sunset."

Albert continued as if uninterrupted. "We have a letter of permission, Miss Sterling—"

"Oh, call me Ruby, do. It's ever so nice of you to stop by. I could give you an audition right here. I—"

"However," the man continued once again, "your mother is loath to part with Miss Ashton's things."

"Oh, who cares about an old Mrs. Grundy like Cinder. It's not like she ain't got herself in hot water now."

As if playing "who can command Ruby's attention more," Mrs. Smith interjected, "Ruby, I must insist—"

"Mother! If you don't let off, he'll get on his high-hat, and I'll never have a chance at Sunset Studios. Just scram!"

A slow smile spread across the woman's face. With slow, deliberate movements, she began clapping. "Brava, my dear. Excellent performance. I almost missed my cue. Sorry, darling." Mrs. Smith turned to Albert. "You see, Mr. Cohen, the girls have learned that they must take every opportunity as it arises, or they find themselves without any worthwhile ones."

Ruby shifted from incensed to a sweet smile and a curtsy so genuine looking that Gary was inclined to believe it. After the faintest clearing of her mother's throat, the girl said, "And Mother is perfectly correct, of course. We would not wish to be accused of failing to hand over some beloved trinket or another. No, Miss Ashton will just have to retrieve her own belongings… when she can."

Pulling another paper from his pocket, Gary said, "She's given me a comprehensive list of what she believes will be found in her room." He began reading, "Four day dresses—blue, pink, brown, and green. Three skirts—"

Mrs. Smith rose to take the list from him, but Gary didn't like the look in her eye. He pocketed it instead. "If you'll accompany me to her room, I would be happy for you and Mrs. Cohen to ensure we only take what is on this list." A pat to the pocket was meant to reinforce his assertion, because Gary suspected if he handed over that list, he'd never see it again. "Shall we?"

"Once again, I say. I cannot allow anyone but Miss Ashton to leave with her belongings. That is, unless the police request something. I've been told that is a possibility."

Ruby shot a look at her mother. "It is? Why?"

"We'll discuss the whims of jurisprudence some other time, dear. I believe that, as we cannot help our guests, they may prefer to leave."

With a shrug and a sway that likely turned many eyes, Ruby slipped her arm through Gary's and led him to the door, chattering all the way. "We're all sorry Cinder got pinched, of course, but the word's out that she was a torpedo for Mr. Walker—to bump you off and make a lot of dough."

That just might be the most slang I've ever endured from one sentence.

THE CAR WAS empty by the time Gary and the Cohens made their way back across the street to the waiting vehicles. He gave the area a quick scan, but nothing. Disappointment settled in his gut. *You knew he'd probably run.*

Sometimes being right was more bitter than the worst medicine.

A flash in his peripheral vision sent him spinning to see what it was, but Gary saw nothing. Seconds later, the passenger door opened, and Herbie dove in beside him. "I think they saw me. Go!"

While he pushed the button to start the car, Gary glanced at the front door of the boarding house. No one stood on the porch—no silhouette in the door. However, motion to the left showed lace curtains fluttering. *The breeze or someone watching?* It didn't matter. Herbie hadn't done anything wrong—that Gary knew of, anyway.

"What were you doing over there?" Gary asked as he pulled out and headed for their next destination.

"When I saw the girl come in, I went to see if'n I could listen after you left. Hear what they said. Thought it'd take a might longer'n it did, though. That girl weren't actin'. She gave her mama what for and how!"

Gary would've put good money on that being true if he'd been a betting man. "Suspect you're correct."

"That rhymes—like songs and po'try but isn't all fancified. I like it." After Gary turned toward Beverly Hills and away from Gary's apartments, Herbie asked, "Where're we goin'?"

"We think it's time to see Mr. Walker. A few… *insinuations* and outright accusations have been made about these murders. We also need to see if he's ever hired the Sterling-Smith girls."

"He'd be a fool. Those dames are meanness in skirts and beads. Why, they even made Cindy iron their clo's and such."

Although he could imagine Lucinda agreeing to assisting the Smiths—after all, the girl personified kindness and helpfulness—he couldn't imagine anyone *making* her do anything she didn't care to do. Her gentle demeanor belied a steel will when urged to do what she thought wrong or crossed her own preferences.

Saying as much seemed a poor way to urge the boy to be forthcoming, so Gary only turned onto another street and said, "Indeed?"

"Oh, yeah. That Ruby's a spiteful one. When Cindy didn't agree to clean up an ashtray that Ruby threw against a wall, she found her little goldfish dead on th' table—*outside the bowl.* Got scolded for the watermark on th' table, too. Mrs. Smith added a dollar to the rent for it."

Did Cinda say that helping the girls into the theater through the back door was Ruby's idea? Had she been home when Cinda was locked in the cellar? Could Ruby *have shot…? Not for Walker, surely, but maybe out of spite…?*

But, of course, she couldn't have. She was in the theater for at least two—likely all three—of the shots. Anyone near her would have known.

"What're you thinkin' up, Mr. Prince?"

"Not to disillusion you, Herbie, but it's Prinz—like zebra at the end there. Prince was just Mr. Walker's idea."

"Is your name Garrison?"

He shook his head. "That was Mr. Walker's idea, too. I guess because it sounded more sophisticated than plain old Gary. Although what is sophisticated about a group of troops, I don't know. Might as well call me guard or something."

"Guard? What for?"

Facetiousness is wasted on children. I wonder if Jesus' admonition to become like little children extends to plain speech and avoiding things like facetiousness and sarcasm.

"Mr. Prinz?" The boy giggled. "Sounds funny. Prinz."

"Oh, guard. Only that it also started with G and had similar military and police connotations."

"Then all the ladies'd've tried to handcuff you. *They*'d've been the p'lice."

How can a child be so proficient in slang and so abysmal at simple English?

"That's an unfortunate way to refer to an engagement ring."

"All the fellas says it. I hear 'em talkin' sometimes when I shines shoes an' such."

And your grammar is all over the place. Correct one moment and lousy the next. That thought prompted another one. "I imagine swells tip better the more uneducated you sound, don't they?"

Herbie shot him a grin. "Can't say I knows the right way to talk all the time, but Ma allus said to play to your strengths. Mine's makin' folks like me."

"It's a good strength to have. Worked on me, and it sounds like Cinda, too."

"But I really like her. She's swell. Keen, too." Herbie watched Gary's reaction at the next stop as Gary waited for a large car to maneuver out of the way.

Gary couldn't argue with that. "Lucinda is lovely, isn't she?" Taking a chance, he shot the boy a look. "Can you keep a secret?" The car lurched forward when Gary let off the clutch too quickly. Nearly stalled as well.

"Sure. I keeps lots of 'em."

"I was going to ask her to marry me today."

Nothing could have prepared him for the tirade that followed. Half the words made no sense, but eventually several emerged clearly enough for him to riddle out the rest. "Whoa… who said anything about thinking she was guilty? Are we not driving to question someone who might know who *is*? Would I be doing that if I thought *she* was?"

Herbie grunted something that Gary took as agreement that the idea wasn't likely.

The Cohens pulled into Walter Walker's estate, Traumwood, and Gary shot up the drive as well. Reporters raced behind them, but a man stepped from the imposing doors of the mansion and ordered the press off the property. Even as the men backed away, they shouted questions, and one enterprising young man tried to snap a photograph—one that couldn't possibly be worth anything between the overcast sky and all the movement.

If Gary were honest with himself, he'd admit that he expected to be escorted off the premises with even less ceremony. Mr. Cohen, however, took care of that. "I'd like to see Walter, Davies."

Davies gave a slight inclination of his head and requested they follow him. Usually, Gary would expect to be shown the terrace with its fine view of the ocean, but with the rain threatening to return at any moment, he rather doubted it.

Walker's "study" opened out onto that terrace, but the doors stood closed as Davies led them into the room and announced their arrival in his quiet tones. Walker turned, nodded at Albert Cohen, began to greet Miriam, and nearly exploded at the sight of Gary. "What are *you* doing here? Isn't ruining me enough? Now you're here to, what? Gloat? Get out of my house!"

"Gary is here at my request."

While the men verbally circled each other before either could decide when and how to throw the first word-punch, Gary glanced around him, aware for the first moment that Herbie had not followed them into the house. *What is he up to…?*

"And why are *you* here?" Walker said at last.

"Accusations."

The man went gray and shot a look at Gary. "What accusations?"

"It has been reported that you hired someone to try to kill Gary in order to sensationalize his death for profit."

"Libel! Slander! I'll sue!"

Miriam Cohen interrupted. "Gentlemen, before we turn this into a schoolyard brawl, may I suggest we all be seated?" She smiled at Walker. "Would Davis be so kind as to arrange for coffee? It's dismal enough to call for something bracing, don't you think?"

"I don't have anything stronger, if that's what you're insinuating."

Albert stepped forward. "Insult my wife again and you'll need something stronger."

"Insult—?"

"Boys!" Laughter bubbled over as Miriam removed a fox stole from around her neck and dropped it over the arm of the couch before settling into it. When they didn't follow suit, she wiped every trace of mirth from her demeanor and ordered, "Sit *down*."

To Walker's credit, he did call for Davies, he did request coffee, sandwiches, and cake, and he did apologize. "It's been brutal. The press won't stop calling, the police won't stop barging in and demanding answers to questions that make no sense, and my wife wants me to bail out that cigarillo girl tomorrow. She's decided the girl's innocent."

Gary couldn't keep quiet at that. "She's right."

"Not in my house," Walker snapped. "Keep your opinions to yourself."

Without missing a beat, Albert said, "And you were where when that first shot was fired?"

Though he would have spoken for Walker—would have said, "Three rows ahead of us—two seats to the left of Helen" —Gary snapped his jaw shut. The scene flashed in his memory as if a photographer had taken a snapshot with flashing powder.

He relived it again. The house lights flickering and burning bright, and Gary shifting his gaze from Eva beside him to where Cinda would be walking toward them. There was only one problem.

In his memory, the seat where Mr. Walker had been sitting was empty.

FOURTEEN

Sterile. Lucinda hadn't expected the courtroom to be sterile, but it was. The judge's bench, the rows of seats, the lack of windows… Of course, if she'd been asked, she wouldn't have been able to describe what she expected. She'd never expected to see the inside of a courtroom. Ever.

She sat on the bench beside two others, wearing the new blue dress Mrs. Cohen had brought her, and with her hair brushed and pinned in place. One by one, the judge listened to the charges, asked a few questions, and either set a bail amount—lower than she imagined they'd set for her—or denied bail. *That'll be me. Denied.*

Although Mrs. Cohen and Gary had both insisted she had nothing to worry about, nothing about releasing an accused murderer made sense to her, bail or no bail. What were even thousands of dollars compared to a life? "*We'll pay the bail,*" Mrs. Cohen had insisted, despite all of Cinda's objections.

"Miss Lucinda Ashton."

She rose as the others before her had done. "Yes, your honor?"

The judge read the complaint against her, and Mr.

Darrow rose. To her surprise, although Lucinda didn't know why she should be, the judge acknowledged the man and asked him to state his business. "I'd like to request that all charges be dismissed for insufficient evidence."

After looking over spectacles at both the lawyer and Lucinda and back at the papers in his hands, he said, "Her shoe was found at the scene of the crime?"

"A shoe she was not wearing, sir. She left the building in the presence of two witnesses, who are present in this courtroom today, wearing both shoes. Furthermore, she was in the presence of witnesses for all but just a minute or two at most —not enough time to get through the back of the building, kill someone, go out the back, lose a shoe, and return wearing both shoes."

The judge looked back at his papers. "The complaint doesn't mention witnesses. Today isn't about presenting evidence, Mr. Darrow. We're here to—"

Doors banged from the back, and a few people seated around the room began murmuring. A man strode into the room, his shoes creating sharp echoes with each footfall, and the judge waved him forward. Once he perused a paper the man held out, the judge then peered over his spectacles, looking first at the man, then Mr. Darrow, and over to Lucinda before stating, "Case withdrawn. Next… that would be Eddington…"

What else the man said, Lucinda didn't hear. She found herself enveloped in a hug and led from the courtroom to a loud murmur of voices and the banging of a gavel with demands for order that went unheeded. As the doors shut behind her, reporters clamored for a response, but Mr. Darrow promised to make a statement once "Miss Ashton has been taken away. She is, as you can imagine, under a great deal of shock and strain."

"Will she give an interview later?"

"That remains to be seen."

More questions were fired at them, one after the other. Did she know why the district attorney had withdrawn the case? Did she know who had killed the three victims and shot another? Was she guilty?

That one prompted her to gasp, "Of course, not!" before she could stop herself, but Mr. Darrow didn't react. He just led her to the car, opened the door, and ushered the ladies in. Mr. Cohen slipped in on the other side, and when she looked back, she saw Mr. Darrow standing there, speaking with the horde of newspapermen.

"What will he tell them? I don't even know the answers—except to whether I am guilty, of course."

"He'll make a ten-minute statement to the effect of, 'They had no evidence, and they knew it. She shouldn't have been arrested.' That'll give us time to get home before any of them hope to get there, which is all he's trying to do."

"Will Gary be…?" She bit her lip and shook her head. "It's probably best—"

Mrs. Cohen patted her hand and squeezed it before giving Lucinda a bit of space again. "He's gone to Pasadena to buy that house you looked at the other day."

"Oh."

"He took Herbie with him."

That dragged her back out of the funk she'd slipped into. "Herbie? Really? How—?"

The story came out—how Gary had met the boy, taken him with them to the boarding house, overheard enough to make Gary suspicious, and then had ridden to the Walker place with them. "While we were inside trying to discern if the accusations against Walter were valid, that boy sneaked over to the garage and rummaged through the cars in there looking for anything like evidence."

"What evidence did he expect to find?"

Mr. Cohen spoke when his wife choked with… well, some kind of emotion. Lucinda wasn't certain what. "He didn't know, but the boy found a gun—handgun. What he describes sounds like a Mauser, but I'd have to see it to be certain." Only in that word, *Mauser*, did Lucinda hear the faintest trace of a German accent.

He'd know, I guess. Wasn't he born there? Her throat dried faster than a dewdrop in Death Valley in July. "Mr. Walker's?" she choked out.

"Can't know," Mr. Cohen admitted. "It was found under the driver's seat. Was it shoved under from the back? Kept there by the driver? We don't know, but Darrow's putting a word into the D.A.'s ear."

Something about it didn't sound right. "But Mauser sounds German."

"It is." Mr. Cohen stared at her. "Why?"

"Well…" She swallowed hard. "Mr. Walker wasn't in the war—didn't fight for Germany. How would he get a German gun?"

It happened again—that awful tightness that came when she saw something familiar that reminded her of her parents. The Cohens exchanged one of those silent looks that long-married people did when they had something to say that didn't need words. Mrs. Cohen patted her hand again and said, "His son fought in the war, though. Came home a local hero, remember?"

"But—"

"Lots of soldiers brought back souvenirs from France and Germany. Trinkets, small bits of art or pottery—"

Mr. Cohen broke in there. "And guns they'd taken from soldiers they'd captured."

The car pulled into the Cohens' estate drive, and Lucinda's heart skipped all the way to the waiting Studebaker and the two fellows leaning against it. Grinning.

"Gary!"

By the time Mrs. Cohen had extracted herself from the backseat and made room for Lucinda to slide out, Gary had reached the door as well. In a move that belonged in a movie, she stepped out of the vehicle and into his arms. "Cinda…"

"They withdrew the case!"

"Give me a minute," he whispered. "I just want to hold you for a minute."

Eyes closed, head resting against his shoulder, Lucinda relaxed and allowed herself to revel in a moment she'd begun to doubt could ever happen.

As if the previous day hadn't given every impression of an omen of impending doom, California's famous sunshine beamed down on them as Gary lingered just a moment longer. She was safe. The temptation to propose before something else happened to prevent him almost overrode Gary's desire to create something special they'd always remember. *The beach, I think. Perhaps the Santa Monica pier—something different from the dinner this mess stole from her.*

Only a few birds singing in the rustling leaves of nearby trees marred the silence. "I think a few of our avian friends are celebrating with me."

"Our—oh!" Cinda leaned away from him, scanning the area. Her cheeks turned pink before deepening into a dark rose. "I think we've been abandoned."

She stepped back, and Gary decided. *Today.* A moment later, he added to that thought, *Now.* However, Cinda had already turned to go inside. "We shouldn't keep them waiting. Not after—"

"Cinda…?"

Those honey waves begged to be freed from their pins.

Hers were natural waves that, when not working, she didn't arrange into the fashionable Marcel style. He preferred that natural look but hadn't ever told her. With one step toward her, he reached for a hairpin that just peeked out from behind an ear and plucked it from her head. "You don't need this, do you?"

"Gary!"

He reached back, felt for another, and plucked it from her head. "Or this?"

"What on *earth*?" Cinda's hand flew to the back of her head, but Gary was quicker. He snatched another one from the other side, and when she tried to stop him, reached up and grabbed the last he could see.

Hair began tumbling down around her shoulders. Gary smiled at the astonished and, if he were truthful with himself, piqued look she gave him. Once more, he slid an arm around her waist and drew her close. "I really do dislike hairpins, you know."

Caught off guard once again, Cinda dropped her forehead to his chest and stammered out, "What'll the Cohens think?"

Given the opportunity, he managed to find another pin before she caught on. "Why should they think anything but that you enjoy your hair down and free… as I do."

Shoulders shaking, Cinda buried her head into his chest again as gasps and… A new thought slammed into him. *Are they sobs?*

"Cinda? I'm sorry. I didn't mean—" He broke off when she stepped back, and the muffled sounds exploded from her. Laughter.

"You—you're the—" More laughter. "—silliest man ever." Shoulders still shaking, she withdrew a few pins he couldn't see and pressed them into his hand before shaking out her hair.

Just watching the waves tousled by the movement and the

breeze solidified his decision. "You stay right here." He angled her a smidge as if an artist choosing the best light and pose. "Yes. Just like that. I'll be back in a jiffy."

"But Gar—"

"Do you trust me, Cinda?"

Only love could create such an instant transformation from objection to a smile. Still, his heart swelled at her quiet, confident, "Yes. Of course, I do."

"I'll be right back."

Jervis met him at the door, an uncharacteristic smile on his face, too. "It's good to see her again, sir."

"Will you tell the others that we'll be back in… oh, a couple of hours at least." He smiled at the man's unquestioning nod. "As champagne isn't permitted these days, perhaps they'd have bottles of ginger ale ready. We may, Lord willing, have more than one cause for celebration."

"I'll let Martha know. She'll bake a cake, I'm sure."

That settled, Gary rushed back to Lucinda, helped her into the Studebaker, and jogged around to his side. Once in, he did something he'd thought about, agonized over, and even dreamed of. Gary leaned over, slid an arm around her shoulders, and tugged her closer. "Sit with me."

The pink returned to Cinda's cheeks, but she didn't refuse. In one graceful move, she slid to his side and, while too self-conscious to look at him, the smile on her face told him he'd pleased her. *Ten miles. I have to find some way to fill ten miles. Then what? Sand and beach? The carousel?*

Miles flew past at a swift, thirty-five miles-per-hour clip, and Gary need not have worried about filling the time with words. Before they'd made it out the gates, Cinda slipped a hand around his arm and leaned against his shoulder. *Bliss.*

The outline of the Whirlwind Dipper coaster slowly emerged on the horizon. *Almost there.* Cinda turned to look at him, and only the fact that they were zipping along at breakneck speed kept him from taking the opportunity to kiss her.

"Are we going to the pier? The Pleasure Pier at Santa Monica?"

"I thought—"

She shifted away from him, but Gary could still feel her stare—or was it a glare? "Our new friends have just helped me escape a trial for a crime I didn't commit, and you're taking me to… what? A fun house? Gary!"

A tenth of a mile passed. Two. With arms folded across her chest, Cinda stared out through the windshield, but she didn't move any further away. As he neared the pier, the perfect response—he hoped, anyway—came to him. "Cinda, I thought you said you trusted me."

Once more, he felt her gaze on him. That same hand slipped around his arm. Her cheek rested against his shoulder again even as she inched closer once more. "You're right. I said that and I meant it. I guess I just don't understand why you'd do…"

The way she trailed off hinted she'd realized his intention. Cinda occasionally spoke as if she didn't consider herself to be all that bright, but Gary had often disagreed. She could be naive at times, certainly. However, Cinda had more common sense and intuition than most people he knew. How had she not guessed his plans before they exited the Cohen's estate?

Mental exhaustion and likely lack of sleep, his mind suggested. *And you're contributing to more of each with your impatience—most likely, anyway.*

"The shore, the Whirlwind Dipper, or the carousel? Which first?"

"I've never been on a roller coaster before. Should we do that first in case it unsettles my stomach? I'd have time to recuperate a bit before we got back in the car…"

And a fellow can't propose on a rattly, clattering coaster anyway. He parked, hopped out of the car, and jogged around to open her door. If he stood a little close and gazed at her for a moment, it surely could be forgiven. Couldn't it?

"I'm so glad you're out of there. And safe," Gary added. He started to tell her about the house, but his more temperate side suggested he wait. *I could drive her over. Why not? She'd think we were hurrying back at first.*

A quavering smile preceded a, "I knew I'd be safe. You were praying for me. I knew that." That smile nearly did him in. The words did.

Hugging in public—not the done thing, but Gary did it anyway. "We'll find what happened to your shoe so that can't come back on you," he promised. "Now let's go see just how adventuresome your insides are." *How romantic of you, Gary Prinz.*

Nerves showed themselves about the time they got in line. There weren't many people ahead of them, but squealing women and roaring men zipped past. Cinda fidgeted. "It is safe, isn't it? They wouldn't want to risk people getting hurt?"

"I've ridden it several times."

"Well if you can, so can I!"

The bravado lasted until they climbed into the cars and waited for the ride to begin. "Gary…"

"You're safe with me."

"But are *you* safe with me?" A glance at her showed Cinda blushing. "What if I get sick all over you?"

Taking her hand in his, Gary squeezed and whispered, "I'll survive."

Twisting, turning, the car occasionally threw her into him, and Gary did his best not to crush her. Only the Monday lack of crowd allowed them their own car—that and a knowing look from the operator. One last dip, another twist, and the car rolled into place. Head thrown back, eyes sparkling, Cinda laughed and squealed before hugging him. "Thank you! I needed that. It's as if all that rushing wind blew off the doom and gloom of this weekend."

Gary led her away from the coaster and asked, "Still game for a walk on the beach, or do you want the carousel first?"

After a quick survey of the pier, Cinda slipped her hand back into his and said, "The beach. I feel like I might not enjoy the carousel as much immediately after such an exhilarating ride."

"Let's go!"

FIFTEEN

The waves crashed against the shore—large waves that demanded she respect the power of the sea. Lucinda stood, her hand in Gary's, gazing out over the water. "I've never equated the ocean with freedom, but today that's how it feels—free."

Giving her hand a squeeze first, Gary dropped it and began untying his shoes. "Come on. Let's allow the water to freeze our toes."

"But—" Her cheeks heated, but Lucinda forced herself to whisper, "I can't, Gary. I'm wearing stockings."

He swept the beach with one hand. "There's no one here for yards and yards."

No one but you and anyone on the pier.

"I'll turn my back… shield you. The girls at school used to manage to shimmy their stockings down without lifting their skirts much if at all above the knee…"

I'm discussing stockings with a man. Will this be normal soon? Will we argue over how much is too much to spend replacing them? Will he tease me about preferring silk over rayon? Will he tease me about how often I have to darn the heels and toes?

"I'd threaten to do it for you, Cinda, but we both know I don't have that right…"

The unspoken "yet" unsettled her enough to turn her back on him and fumble through her skirt for the clasps on her garter. The fronts weren't difficult, but she elbowed him twice in the backside, much to her mortification, attempting to unhinge those back clasps. Rolling them down… "I never imagined I'd be so fast and modern as to roll my stockings!"

"Are those toes ready for some salty frostbite?"

After stuffing her stockings into her shoes, she wriggled her toes in the sand before coming to stand before him. "Ready."

He took the shoes from her hand and set them atop his own. "We'll leave them there. Come on!"

Hand in hand, they raced to the shoreline. The moment her toes hit the damp sand, she squealed. "You weren't teasing! This will be cold!"

"The Pacific in May? Hardly warm at any time of year, but definitely chilly now." He tugged her closer to where the waves stretched icy fingers to touch her toes. "Come on."

"I'll freeze!"

Before she could anticipate his intention, Gary swept an arm around her waist and lifted her, cradling her to his chest. Feet kicking, he strode out into the water, and only then did she realize he'd rolled up his trousers, too.

"Now, Miss Lucinda Ashton," he began as he held her close but perfectly poised to toss her into the waves. "When will you learn to trust me?"

Bold? Her mother would have said so. Her aunt would have scolded her for a month, and Lucinda didn't even want to imagine what her grandmother would have said. However, she did it. She slipped both arms around his neck and rested her cheek against his. "I do." The hitch in his breath told her she'd said the right thing, so she took bold to brazen as she added, "But how else was I to convince you to hold me like this again?"

For long, agonizing, and delightful seconds, Gary just held her there, his arms strong and sure. An uncharacteristic flight of poetic fancy struck Lucinda as time crept past as if on tiptoe, unwilling to disturb them. *It's as if he's carrying me over the threshold—and he is. Everything will change now, even as it stays the same, too.* Gary's voice broke through the fanciful thoughts.

"I know how," he said as he waded back through the receding waves and set her down just out of reach of the tide. One hand fumbled in his pocket.

Lucinda held her breath. *He's really going to do it—even now. Even after…*

"You're not surprised, I hope," Gary said as he found what he'd sought. "I've tried to…" As his gaze met hers, he faltered. "You know I love you, don't you?"

"A girl knows better than to assume, but I've wondered."

He nodded. "You knew why I took you to look at the houses, didn't you?"

"Again…"

Once more, Gary nodded. "A fellow can't just let a girl wait around wondering. I knew I'd have to tell you about my former vocation if I didn't manage to make you notice me that last night. It's why I made so many hints about what I wanted *before* then. So, you'd believe me when I told you that I'd done everything for you. Well, I chose the institute for the Lord, but…"

His hands toyed with a ring—modest stone cut like an emerald, but the green was warmer than that—with brownish and yellowish facets. He held it up. "Do you know how hard it was for me not to give this to you on Friday? It matched that dress so perfectly."

"I chose that dress because I knew you'd say it reminded you of my eyes."

"Which is why I confounded the jeweler when I found this stone. It was part of a display—just scattered in the case as a bauble, but…" He held it up in the light, allowing the colors to shine. "May I put it on?"

Before she could remind him that he hadn't actually asked anything, Gary chuckled. "I should say, 'Will you marry me, Cinda?'"

"Yes, of course!"

"*Now*, I'll ask again."

He didn't have to. Lucinda stuck her hand out and nearly shoved her finger right into the ring in the process. "Tell me about the jeweler," she said as she admired the sparkle of the stone against her hand. "How did you confound him?"

"Well, he knew who I was, of course. I could afford anything in the store as far as he was concerned. But I went from admiring a ruby—that verse in Proverbs, you know—to seeing that stone. After that, nothing else would do." His hand covered hers. "I've no doubt he cheated me on the setting and the price of the stone, but I decided that I could indulge in one bit of reckless spending—for you."

Lucinda didn't even try to hide joy that wouldn't be repressed. She flung arms around his neck, kissed his cheek, held him fast. "Thank you," she whispered. "And I'm sorry I was so… difficult and cross about you not telling me who you are. Well, who you *were*."

As he held her close, she could feel the beat of Gary's heart—slow… steady… strong. "I wondered sometimes," he admitted. "I wondered if you were teasing me or punishing me for not telling you at first, but if you were, you'd have been the greatest actress I've ever seen."

Shyness overtook her brief lapse into boldness. Lucinda stepped back, eyes lowered as she ordered her cheeks to stay cool and… and failed. It didn't deter him. Gary took each of her hands in his, one at a time. The way his eyes couldn't stay long off her lips, she knew what to expect… she thought.

Gary bent to kiss her, and the wind laughed and tossed her hair between their lips. He chuckled, brushing it out of the way without ever releasing her hand. However, as his lips finally touched hers, Lucinda Ashton discovered just how unexpected Gary Prinz's, *her fiancé*'s, kiss actually was. Somewhere between that first meeting of their lips and the moment he stepped back and gave her a sheepish grin, Lucinda managed to choke out an, "I love you, too, Gary."

Once he had a yes, all of Gary's mind became fixated on preparing for a wedding—first up, admit he hadn't bought the house she expected him to. "Let's ride the carousel. Then I need to show you something."

"Can we ride it another day?" Lucinda buried her toes in the sand. "We really should get back to the Cohens. I need to thank them, and I'd like to take a *real* bath. I feel filthy."

"We can, but…" He'd have to tell her. "I need to show you your wedding present."

"We're not married yet."

Gary took her hand and led her back to their shoes. "No, but I bought your gift today, nonetheless. *Someone* insisted I not attend the hearing, so what else was I to do?"

"But—"

"Albert knows my plans. Or…" Gary amended as he realized they'd only spoken around the plans—not actually stated them. "I believe he does. He hinted that you'd need good news, and I told him about the gift."

By that point, Lucinda seemed to have understood what the gift would be. "Oh…"

"Let's go."

Of course, she likely didn't know it would take a solid three-quarters of an hour to get there. Once there, they'd need to find something to eat before returning to the Cohens' house. Still, driving all the way to Pasadena, one arm around her shoulder whenever he didn't have to change gears—could anything be sweeter after having her released from police custody?

She flicked a finger at her skirt. "It was kind of Mrs. Cohen to bring me this dress, but I'll be happy to get back into my own clothes." A gasp followed. "Oh, my room! It must have been a mess when you went. I'd just gotten out of the cellar and dashed to change—couldn't find anything. I flung things here and there…."

"We never made it to your room. Mrs. Smith wouldn't allow it."

"Whyever not?"

Gary pulled onto Chester Avenue and pulled up in front of the Craftsman he and Herbie had finally decided on just that morning. "We're here."

"Here?" Cinda glanced around. "This doesn't look like what…"

Turning to her, he took one of her hands in his. "Look… I've done something that I hope won't annoy you. Based on things you've said…" He kissed her cheek and bolted from the car. By the time he made it to the passenger door, she'd slid over, ready to exit.

"Gary, I don't think I understand."

"I brought Herbie with me today. He stayed at my apartment last night and we talked. Then on the way here this morning, I told him about an idea I had, and… Cinda, I had to. I could see he wanted me to say it, so I did."

She looked first at the house, back at him, and a spark of hope flickered in her eyes. "Gary, what did you say?"

"I told him if he'd agree to behave, help you around the house, go to church with us on Sundays, and do his very best in school, he could live with us—be a Grant or a Prinz, I didn't care which as long as he'd let me practice being a father on him while I wait for the Lord to give me the chance with my—" He grinned despite himself. "*Our* children."

"He agreed?"

Gary nodded and pulled the house key from his other pocket. "We bought this one instead of the other you and I agreed to on Friday. It has another bedroom and a decent-sized room downstairs that'll work for a study, so we won't be underfoot as I try to get him ready for classes. He can read and do sums faster than lightning in his head, but other than that…"

Unease filled his gut as Lucinda glanced first at him, over at the house, and back at him. Then she snatched the key from his hand, grabbed it—his hand, that is—and marched him up the walk, up the steps, and to the door. With some fumbling, trembling fingers being the cause, she managed to get it open and jerk him inside. There, Lucinda kissed him soundly.

"I most *definitely* love you, Mr. Prinz. I'd never have asked, but I've wanted to take in Herbie since the day I met him. Mrs. Smith refused, of course."

Despite the house waiting for her inspection, Gary couldn't resist just one more kiss… and then another.

THEY SPENT the drive back to Beverly Hills discussing wedding plans. He wanted a church, a bouquet for her, a white dress, a veil. She wanted a cake and a light luncheon after a quick trip to City Hall. It took some doing, but Gary managed to get her to agree to a compromise. They'd get married at a small church that she'd attended from time to time before meeting him—one near the boarding house. She'd wear that white dress and veil, and she'd carry that bouquet. There would be a reception following at his apartment—a full brunch with cake.

"How is this a compromise? You're getting everything you wanted."

"As are you—almost. Just the location and really, it's your church…"

He hopped out of the car and jogged around to open her door before she could protest. Herbie bolted out of the house with Jervis strolling sedately behind. “Didja axe her?”

“I asked, if that’s what you mean.”

The boy pounced on Cinda’s ring. “Oh, Miss Cindy, that’s swell!”

“I saw the house you chose for me.”

“Didja like it? Huh? It’s the berries, ain’t it?”

She hugged the boy and Gary could have sworn he heard her say, “If you’re going to live with me, you’re going to give ‘ain’t’ the bum’s rush.”

The boy howled. “Ain’t—I mean, *aren’t* you full of surprises! Never heard you talk slang a’fore.” Without a hint of remonstrance, he changed his own word to “before.”

Jervis stood off to the side, waiting patiently, but only when Gary took a second look did he realize why. He turned to Herbie. “I don’t think Jervis realizes that you’ve traded in your life of crime for a home with me. Would you assure him that you’ll not touch or take anything without permission?”

Herbie winked at Gary before turning to Jervis. “Bet you’ve been runnin’ your dogs off. Well, I ain’t—am not—takin’ anything that… *isn’t* mine. I promise.” As if an afterthought, he added, “Hardly ever did anyway. Ain’t right.”

The man nodded first at Gary and then at Herbie. “Very good, sir. I’ll leave you in peace then.” Jervis turned to Cinda and added, “Very nice to see you here and well, miss. Would you care for a bath?”

“*Please*. Thank you.”

“Mrs. Cohen has laid out a few things in your room. Do you recall how to find it?”

With a nod Cinda dashed up the steps and into the house, and for just a minute, Gary winced. *I could have given her a house like this if I’d kept working—still could. But…*

“She looks like she owns the place, don’t she?” Herbie sighed. “Still, I’m glad you bought that other place. I wouldn’t want to live where I can't walk without feeling like I'll ruin sumpin'."

Jervis had already started up the stairs—surprisingly swift for someone with such slow, deliberate movements—when Gary and Herbie entered the house. They found the Cohens on the terrace sipping something Gary suspected wasn't exactly Volstead approved. *Early in the day for that…*

"Is she all right?"

"Went up to take a bath."

Miriam gave him a look that ordered him to be a bit more forthcoming.

"Allow me to rephrase that," Gary said. "*My fiancée* went up to bathe. She'll be down soon to celebrate with us."

Herbie cheered as if he'd just heard the news. Albert rose and slapped his back, congratulating him. Miriam just beamed. As he seated himself, Gary sighed. "Now that this mess with the murders is over—"

"But it's not!" Herbie dashed inside.

"What?" Gary stared after him before asking, "What's he talking about?"

"I suspect the headlines," Albert said. "They were brutal this afternoon."

Brutal was an understatement. When Herbie thrust the paper at him, Gary's gut formed into a rock. CIGARILLO GIRL RELEASED DESPITE NEW EVIDENCE AGAINST HER.

"What?"

As he scanned the article, the Cohens both insisted the article had sensationalized rumors and anonymous, unfounded accusations. "They're looking for a way to drag out this idea until the police come up with another suspect," Miriam insisted.

"Well, they ought to look into Mr. Walker." Gary reread a line near the end. "Still, this anonymous source seems to know a lot about Cinda…" He looked up. "She kept trying to ask about her room at the boarding house. I told her we hadn't gotten her things but not why. I couldn't stand to see her disappointed that she'd have to return."

"She didn't seem unwilling to go back while she was at the police station," Albert argued. "Why would—"

Miriam rose, effectively cutting off her husband's words. "That's right," she said. "She refused to return after we left the burning theater, and then at the jail, she kept saying she wished she were at the boarding house. And…"

The woman began to pace. Five one way, about face. Five the other. Eventually, she spun to look straight at him. "Gary?"

"What is it?"

"When you saw her, she brought it up. Am I correct?"

Gary nodded. "Kept saying she wanted to go back."

"And she said she had a cellmate."

"A rat, yes."

The pacing resumed. Gary shot a look at Albert who shrugged his shoulders and watched his wife. That's when Gary understood. "A rat. Every time I tried to get her to talk about who could have done something or what we were learning, she brought up her cellmate—the *rat*."

"I thought she was going a little crazy," Miriam admitted.

"Well, I certainly am." Albert downed his drink and rose. "Will you tell me what's going on?"

"Lucinda was warning us not to talk, dear. The *police* guard was her 'cellmate.'"

Even as they spoke, the words swirled in his mind. *What did Cinda want from her room? What would be so important—her shoe, of course. But why?*

Gary and Miriam spoke in unison. "We need to go there."

SIXTEEN

Refreshed, Lucinda tripped down the stairs, eager to show off her ring and tell Miriam Cohen all about the darling bungalow Gary had purchased. *If half the houses nearby weren't nearly large enough to be mansions or actual mansions, it would be too large to call it "darling," but comparatively, it is. And really, four bedrooms isn't* that *large—not too much to keep up with the housework myself.*

As she neared the terrace, however, she heard an argument—no, more of a debate, she decided—raging out there. "—couldn't have killed Helen. Eva, yes. But he was surrounded by people when Helen was shot. I'd just looked over that way before they came into the theater again."

"Two murderers?" Mrs. Cohen sounded… doubtful? No, it was more… intrigued. "That could explain why not all the evidence aligns with one person. What if Walker *did* shoot Eva by mistake. Then, a different person, knowing they were looking for someone for the first murder, took advantage of it."

"How?" The question came from Gary. "People don't just show up at a theater with a gun handy in case someone else tries to bump off someone in the audience."

There, Mr. Cohen interjected his own idea. "What if

someone found the gun—hidden after the shooting. The moment arrives and… bang!"

Mrs. Cohen caught sight of her. "Congratulations, Lucinda! Let me see your ring!"

The men poured ginger ale and passed it around. Herbie insisted on calling his "champ-ane" and inhaled enough of the stuff to produce a frightful belch. Gary looked proud and happy enough to burst, and despite her damp hair, Lucinda felt like a princess. *More like a Prinz-ess. Or soon enough, anyway.*

The discussion returned to who might have committed the theater murders the moment they all seated themselves. Lucinda turned to Gary. "So, you didn't retrieve my things? You said Mrs. Smith wouldn't allow it?" She frowned at his nod. "Strange…"

"What is strange?"

"I would have thought she'd want to rent the room out immediately—what with me in jail and all."

"Why did you want to go back to your rooming house, Lucinda?" Mrs. Cohen leaned forward. "You were so against it before the police came."

Should she tell them? Was she crazy? Of course, she was. But did her being crazy mean she wasn't right? That, she didn't know. "I wanted to find my shoes."

Four faces and eight eyeballs turned her way. Herbie found his voice first. "What for? You was wearin' 'em."

"My old pair, yes. I had been breaking in new ones. I'd walk to work in them, swap out for old ones, and walk home. Next week I'd have worn them there and back. But I couldn't find them before I left, so I just wore my old ones."

No one seemed to understand the significance of her words. They still stared at her with blank expressions until Herbie asked, "And…?"

"Well, the detective at the station. He showed me the shoe they found. It's mine."

"We know that, Cinda. That's why they arrested you."

Lucinda turned and waited for him to look at her. To *really* look at her. "Gary, it was my *new* shoe. One of the ones I couldn't find before I left for work."

NEVER HAD Gary felt more ridiculous than the moment Lucinda said the *shoe* was the issue. Of course, it was. He'd just said the same thing not five minutes before. *And even as she explained it, you missed it.*

This time, everyone climbed into his Studebaker, and he shot off for the Smith boarding house. "What should we be looking for?" he asked as he pulled out of the driveway and onto the road down toward Hollywood.

"Well, my other shoe, of course. That would be important, I think." Lucinda frowned. "Um… well, if Ruby were responsible for any of it, surely she'd put everything back in my room. So, we should count my uniforms."

"She's a fool if she did." Gary growled.

Miriam protested. "No. If Ruby Smith is responsible for any of the murders, returning everything to that room would make any claims Lucinda had of missing things suspect."

"Right." Gary's mind raced with possibilities. "So, let's say Ruby put on Cinda's uniform and walked to the theater. She goes in the back where…"

"Joe," Cinda choked out. "Poor Joe."

"Right—Joe saw her. Would she have worn a wig? That hair is too dark…"

Theory after theory exploded at once. She'd worn a wig. Joe was color blind. The brightness from outside had blinded him to her. Herbie put a stop to it all with one word—name, rather.

"Opal."

Cinda gasped. "Of course! Her hair is just a little lighter

than mine. She's closer to my height, too. *She* got in, let Ruby in, and then changed out of my uniform."

Gary heard the doubt in Cinda's voice, and he shared it. That made no sense. "Possibly."

But Herbie piped up. "That's what I'd do. I'd give my clo's to Ruby, come in in Miss Cindy's things—like when others are goin' in so's I wouldn't… stand out. Then, I'd go let in Ruby from one of th' side doors out front. I'd be wearin' a uniform, so no one would notice me—not then while everyone's tryin' to get ta work."

"But why would Ruby put on the uniform?" Cinda shook her head. "It all makes sense until right then."

Not until they pulled up to the boarding house did anyone come up with a credible answer. Albert sounded lost in thought as he said, "Maybe she wanted a reason to be able to talk to people—like Walker and me. People who could get her auditions. If someone invited them to a party, she could always change clothes in the lady's lavatory."

"Right!" Herbie's voice nearly deafened them all. "And when Miss Cindy came in, she had to get out of that uniform before someone noticed. That's why she threatened her—I mean, Miss Cindy—I mean, no. Ruby—"

"We follow you, son." Albert sounded pleased as punch at the boy's logic, and Gary couldn't blame the man. It did make sense.

But as Gary looked back and saw the glower on the lad's face, his gut clenched. "Herbie, I need you to do something for us—something difficult, but probably the most important thing you could do." He winced at the eager expression on the boy's face. "It won't feel like it. In fact, it's going to feel like we're just fooling you, but I mean it. If either of these girls know who is responsible for the murders, it might ensure Cinda's safety. Do you understand?" Even as the boy nodded, Gary knew he understood—really understood.

"I stays here. Watch. Keep outta sight in case you don't come back or sumpin'."

Gary knew his smile probably looked more grim than reassuring, but he hoped his eyes conveyed his trust and the pride that welled up in him. *He'll be like a son.* My *son. I hope Cinda and I have a little girl for him to protect from the bullies and the worthless fellows who come buzzing around…*

"Gary?" Cinda stood next to his window. "Are you ready?"

"Thank you, Herbie," he said as he climbed from the car. It was insufficient, but Gary remembered his own adventure-loving self as a boy. Being left behind had to gall. *But it's true. We need him safe* and *to get help if something goes awry.*

Anyone watching would have thought the Cohens, Lucinda, and Gary were making a casual social call as they strolled up the walk and twisted that old-fashioned door buzzer. The clatter of shoes on stairs preceded the arrival of Ruby herself. The girl gaped at the sight of Cinda. "You!"

"I've come for my things, Ruby."

"Your *things*! How dare you show your face—"

Albert cleared his throat and broke in. "We didn't think we'd need a police escort, but if you would prefer that we request one…"

Although she opened the door at that threat, Ruby didn't stop her tirade. She just shifted it in a different direction. "I cannot believe we must allow a criminal in our house! What will the neighbors think?"

"They'll think," Cinda said with that quiet grace that belied the steel behind her words, "that you are well rid of someone when they see us carrying out my things."

"You should have to forfeit everything after killing those people."

Gary would have protested, but Cinda laid a hand on his arm. "Mrs. Cohen can go with me. We'll be down in just a few minutes. Perhaps you might call a taxi for the Cohens?

I'm afraid my things will fill your back seat. We weren't thinking clearly."

With that, Cinda dashed up the stairs, and Ruby flounced out of the room. Marion hadn't made it halfway up when Cinda came rushing back. "Gary, my room is *empty*. There's *nothing* in there. Not a stray button or scrap of paper. It's all gone!"

THE IMPRINT of her bare room refused to leave Lucinda's mind, even as a whispered debate raged around her. *It looks just as it did the day I moved in. Exactly the same. The bare mattress, the fresh linens at the foot, the hideous antimacassar on the old armchair. I set my suitcase…*

At the thought of her suitcase, Lucinda turned and climbed the stairs once more—*one last time*, she thought. The wallpaper had been sponge cleaned recently. Had she not noticed before, or had they cleaned it since she'd been gone? A glance up and down the hallway showed fairy dust sparkling in sunbeams from the window at the end.

Her doorway still stood open as she'd left it. The ugly antimacassar still stood guard over the back of the chair, while the linens still sat on the mattress. The wardrobe at one corner of the room stood tall—nearly to the ceiling. Lucinda dragged a chair over to it and stood on it. She reached up, patting around on the top until she found them—the tiny bundle of notes Gary had written her over the past six or seven months—all tied together with the length of ribbon she'd purchased for just that purpose.

As she stepped down, Gary's voice nearly sent her back to the top again. "Are those mine?"

"No." She turned in time to see him crestfallen. "They're mine—from you."

That slow smile—the one girls all over America swooned

over—formed on his lips. *That'll be just for me, now.* And in that moment, Lucinda felt sorry for all the girls who had dreamed of meeting him someday.

"I scoffed at one of the girls at work a week ago."

He leaned against the doorjamb and folded his arms over his chest. "Scoffed?"

"Abby said she'd be truly happy if you would just notice her, and I said I didn't understand why everyone raved about you like that."

"You crush my heart."

"Then," she added, stepping just a bit closer. "Abby said, 'Not everyone has a handsome boyfriend who wants to be a seminary student.'" Another step. Another. Lucinda paused just shy of touching him and cocked her head, really looking at him for what might have been the first time. "And neither of us knew we were talking about the same man."

They stood there, gazing at one another until Lucinda couldn't bear the intensity anymore. She glanced away, taking one last look around the room. Gary's rumbling voice—that timbre that only came when he tried to speak low enough for only her to hear. "Is that everything?"

"Yes. I was remembering this room and the first time I came in here with my suitcase. Then I remembered how I kept these in my suitcase for the longest time—in the little silk pocket in the lining. But Ruby said something once that made me wonder if she'd read them, so I began hiding them up there on the wardrobe." She curled the packet against her chest. "She doesn't like high things. Always refuses to stand on a stool when her mother needs something."

"And she fancies herself a starlet." Gary shook his head as he stepped aside for Lucinda to pass. "She would never make it at the studio."

Just as Lucinda turned toward the stairs, she realized the hallway wallpaper had been cleaned as well. Despite the creamy color of the background, it looked brighter, fresher.

The woodwork gleamed. The windows shone. "Mrs. Smith has been scrubbing. I suppose I upset her more than I expected."

"Why do you say that?"

She stopped abruptly at the top of the stairs and might have stumbled, but Gary shot an arm out and pulled her back. Lucinda smiled up at him. "There's something you should understand about women, Gary. We all have something that we do when we're bothered about something. Some ladies eat, others rearrange furniture or weed a garden."

"And Mrs. Smith cleans?"

"Yes." Three steps down, she murmured, "I just wish I knew if she cleaned Friday afternoon or Saturday…"

SEVENTEEN

A wave of tenderness swept over Gary as he heard Cinda muttering something about Mrs. Smith's cleaning fit. *She's had such a hard week, and she's concerned about having upset someone. Someday she'll do something that makes her humanity glare, but times like this, I can't help but wondered if she has already been perfected by Christ.*

In the entryway, the quartet held a conference, whispering about what they should do. Miriam pulled Cinda close, asking where Ruby might have gone. "We need to find your things. Are you sure there's nothing upstairs?"

"Not in my room. I remembered not seeing my suitcase and that reminded me that they probably wouldn't have found these." She hugged the letters to her chest.

Gary had to clench his jaw to repress a grin. Who knew his sensible Cinda was also sentimental? "But the suitcase is definitely gone, so where did Ruby or Mrs. Smith or even Opal—?"

That question died as Cinda shook her head. "They're very careful of Opal. She'd never be expected to do anything like pack a room. They'd send her to the stores or to pay a bill or chat with a new boarder. Watering the flowers out front and minor weeding or even light dusting—that's more Opal's purview."

Miriam asked about an outbuilding—a garage or shed. Cinda admitted there was a garden shed but no garage. "They don't keep a car. The red line covers anything we'd need around here."

That caught Albert's attention. "Did you take the streetcars to the theater the other night?"

"No… Ruby could have. I usually save the fare. It's not too far to walk… usually. Friday, I considered it for a moment but decided I might get there just as quickly if I didn't have to wait." Cinda glanced around her. "I wonder where Ruby went. If we don't hurry, we'll start seeing the other boarders coming in. Things could become awkward."

"I've been thinking…"

All eyes turned to watch Albert.

"Well, that idea about someone taking an opportune moment. No one came into the theater to kill that detective."

Gary had to agree the idea seemed impossible.

"That was a murder of perceived necessity or something similar. The first one has to be the planned one, but…" He glanced around him before adding in an even lower tone, "What if someone decided to 'help' the situation somehow—divert suspicion or even to complicate the case?" When no one responded, he explained. "Gary said that Walker wasn't in his seat at the time of the first shot, although he had been earlier. What if Walker *did* kill Eva, trying to shoot Gary?"

Miriam picked up the narrative there. "Then, if Ruby knew it, perhaps she, in an attempt to ingratiate, protect, blackmail…"

"That would explain his behavior at Traumwood." Albert took his wife's arm. "We'll go talk to him. Now that Cinda has been released, he has to know they'll come after him. Perhaps he's being blackmailed. You get her things."

"How will you get to his place?" Cinda sounded panicked.

"We should have brought two cars. This was foolish. What if—?"

"No time for that," Miriam insisted. She patted both Cinda's and Gary's arms, gazing from one to the other. "Just get her things and get out of here. We'll try to get a confession out of Walter and send the police the minute we know something."

Gary and Cinda watched from the door until the couple was out of sight. He gazed at his car but saw no sign of Herbie. "I hope he's all right."

"He's a smart boy. He'll be fine. Let's get my things and go. I'll find Ruby."

"Ruby is right here."

They turned to find Ruby Smith holding a gun pointed straight at Cinda.

"You stupid girl. Always sticking your prissy nose where it doesn't belong."

Beside him, Cinda stiffened and would have protested, but Gary squeezed her elbow in a silent plea for her not to respond. She relaxed. Maybe it would be foolish, but he had to try to get Ruby to put down the gun. "We're not here to hurt anyone, Miss Smith."

"*Sterling!*"

"Just so, *Miss* Sterling. We're here to retrieve Cinda's belongings and let you be."

To his relief, she lowered the gun a couple of inches. A shot could still be fatal, but it didn't look aimed for Cinda's heart any longer.

"I must protect my mother. But if you want Cinder's junk, you can clear it out, I suppose."

"Thank you. Where would we find it? The shed out back?"

Ruby had stepped aside for them to pass toward the kitchen and the back door, but once they entered the narrow hallway to the kitchen, she said. "No, no. Too filthy out there.

We take care of our boarders' possessions—even if they turn out to be criminals like Cinder here. They're in the cellar."

Ahead of him, Cinda shuddered, and no wonder. "I'll just go on down and retrieve them. There's a suitcase and… a box or a crate or two?"

"She's a packrat, this one. All sorts of doodads and gewgaws. A packed suitcase—we tied a rope around it so it wouldn't burst. Three boxes and a crate."

"Labeled?"

With an indifferent shrug, Ruby opened the cellar door. "I don't know what Mother did with them. I don't go down there." A high-pitched giggle escaped. "But Cinder does."

The glee in the girl's tone shifted to steel as the gun rose again. "She'll have to help you."

"If we step into that cellar, you're going to shut the door on us," Cinda protested. "You can't imagine that we're that gullible—not again."

"Of course, you're not. We underestimated you. Everyone thought you were just a Mrs. Grundy, but you weren't. Just another gold digger, aren't you? Found yourself a daddy and—"

"You don't have to insult my fiancée," Gary protested. "She didn't even know who I was—"

But Cinda interrupted him. "We don't owe her an explanation or a refutation of her erroneous assertions, Gary."

While Gary had never considered Cinda to be undereducated, her vocabulary tended toward the pedestrian. Hearing her throw out a sentence like that—heavy-handed with the word choice—confused him until he saw Ruby equally confused. *She doesn't know what you said.*

"Never mind all that." The girl waved the gun with reckless abandon. "Get a wiggle on."

Locked in the cellar might be safer out of range of that gun. "Of course. When can we expect to be released? Before or after our friends return with the police?"

"Police!"

"Someone shot four people on Friday, and they want to know who did it."

The girl's head wagged as if controlled by a force outside herself. "No, no. Only three shots fired. Only three." Her gaze darted from Gary to Cinda, and back to Gary again. "I didn't kill anyone!"

"And we didn't accuse you of it, but we think you know something about what happened. After all, you weren't supposed to be there, but you were."

It had been the wrong thing to say. Ruby aimed once more. "Get down there."

"Ruby—"

She swung to where Cinda took a step forward, trying to calm her. Her eyes flashed and her voice went cold again. "*Go!*"

Cinda turned and started for the stairs, but Gary chose to go first. "I'll make sure everything is all right. Turn on a light. Then you—"

He hadn't made it three steps down when Cinda screeched and tumbled into his back. He stumbled. Hands gripping the rickety railing, he felt it give way, but it had helped break his fall. Cinda, half past him, kept going even as they heard a bolt slide into place. He reached out one hand to grab her, but all he managed to do was slow her progress down to the floor.

Muffled words followed from above. "She was just trying to help! I couldn't let him kill her, could I?"

ONE MOMENT she'd started to take her first step down, ready to call out to tell Gary where to find the light chain, and the next, Lucinda felt a shove to her back. Arms flailing, she heard a horrible screech—one that misnamed western owls would have envied. The moment she collided with Gary, Cinda realized the screech came from her.

That collision halted her forward projection for only a moment. Gary grabbed for her, but she slipped from his grasp and skidded headfirst down the wooden steps to the floor. Her head hit the ground at the same time the clatter of his feet followed her down the stairs. From above, Ruby shouted something, but the instant pounding in her head and the clattering of his feet made it impossible for Lucinda to hear.

"Are you all right?" Gary's foot landed on her ankle, and he, too, went down. She heard a crack that sounded painful.

"Are *you* all right?"

"Sounds worse than it is. I have a knee that pops." Despite his cheerful words, Gary sounded a bit… pinched. "But you?"

"Scraped, I think. Hit my head. Probably ruined this dress. She tried to stand and sat down hard. "Twisted an ankle and dropped my letters, too." Perhaps it wasn't the right time to ask, but Lucinda couldn't help it. "What did Ruby say?"

"Something about how she was only trying to help."

Then had it been as Mr. Cohen said? Ruby had done something that night. "Did she say she hadn't killed anyone?"

"Yes." His shuffles told her he was trying to do something but what Lucinda couldn't imagine. "Where's that blasted chain?"

A spider crawled across her hand, and Lucinda screeched again. "I thought I killed you last time!"

"What?"

"Spider!"

His rumbling chuckle annoyed her, but not nearly as much as his, "I wouldn't have taken you for one squeamish about spiders."

"I don't mind *seeing* them, but feeling them in the dark…" A shudder rippled through her.

Gary's hand touched her hair. "Cinda? If I help, could you stand?"

"I think so. I don't think it's a bad wrench."

Supporting her first as she stood and then as she limped, he shuffled her one way and then another until he cried, "Eureka!"

"What have you found?"

"The stairs. I thought you could sit on a step. I'm afraid of stepping on you again."

Of course. It wasn't wrenched, just bruised. "Forgot about that. I'll probably be fine in a few minutes." She lowered herself and felt both ankles. "It might be swollen, but I don't think much if any."

"That's good." Gary's breath wisped across her cheek as he murmured the words. A kiss followed. "I'm sorry, Cinda. I didn't really believe she was dangerous to us. I was a fool."

"I'm not sure she's *dangerous*, as much as..." Lucinda fumbled for the right word. "Well, she seems a little *unbalanced*, doesn't she?"

"That's one way of describing it." Gary's shoes shuffled across the dirt floor as he turned this way and that, trying to reach for the chain. "Who do you think she meant?"

Perhaps Lucinda had hit her head harder than she'd realized. "Who... what?"

"Ruby. She said '*she*' was just trying to help. Who is 'she' do you suppose?"

"Oh!" That put a new kink in the works. "I thought you meant 'she' as in Ruby. Um... Well, I don't—" Of course, she did. It just didn't make sense. "Opal was there, Gary. She has to mean Opal, but I can't imagine that girl being willing to pick up a gun, much less fire it with enough accuracy to hit anyone."

They argued over that one. Gary said she obviously didn't know the Smiths as well as she thought, and Lucinda insisted Opal would be the greatest actress ever born if she could hide her true character *that* well. "Besides. She was in the theater for at least two of the shots. I'm sure of it. I only followed her backstage just before—"

"Just before Detective Lindstrom was shot. If you'd caught up with her, she might have shot you."

"But I'm certain she was out front for the others! Trying to help…" Lucinda dropped her head into her hands and tried to think. "Did she go back thinking Ruby was back there? Could she have thought Ruby did it for… no. I don't believe Ruby shot anyone. She's unsettled enough that I think she'd have told us—even if only by accident. But—"

As if he read her mind, Gary pulled on the light at the same time he said, "Where did they get the gun if they didn't shoot Eva and Helen?"

"Mr. Cohen said Herbie found a gun—a German one—in Mr. Walker's car. Under the seat. What if Mr. Walker gave that gun to Ruby after the theater?"

"It wouldn't have been in his car, then."

A chill ran through her as she said, "Unless he came here today. Or they met somewhere. Or…"

Rattling from the corner turned both heads that direction. Lucinda whispered, "What do you think that is?"

"Don't know. Stay here."

Grasping his hand, she pulled him back. "No… It could be anything—anyone. We should hide just in case."

Only one problem prevented that. There was no place to hide. The cellar wasn't like an attic with nooks and crannies and old piled up things to conceal them. Floor to ceiling shelves lined the walls except beneath the stairs and in one corner. As she looked, she saw her suitcase and the boxes Ruby had mentioned. "There are my things." She pointed high. "Up there."

Gary squeezed her hand for a moment before moving to lift down the suitcase. "It is heavy," he murmured. "Should I worry about you filling our house with all sorts of gimcracks?"

"The gewgaws Ruby referred to will likely make the next

boxes heavy. They're books, most of them. I had to leave my parents' books behind when they died, so when I moved here, I began replacing them as I could afford it."

As if to prove her point, the next box nearly took Gary down with it. He set it on the dirt floor with a *whump!* and settled his hands on his hips with a smirk shot her way. "Will I have to fight you for bookshelf space in my study?"

"Not if you provide enough bookshelf space somewhere else for me."

Though he didn't move an inch nearer, she felt his presence envelop her as he stood there smiling. "But what if I like having you in my study while I'm learning all the ways to use the Greek article?"

"I hope you do—" Lucinda stopped herself. "Did you say that Greek has only one article? As in *A* and *the*? Which one do they have?"

"Yes—no indefinite articles for them. And having twenty-four versions of their definite article, they really didn't have space in their primers for another one."

A giggle escaped despite the circumstances. "I hope you'll like having me in there—if only to bring you coffee and cookies to keep your brain functioning while trying to learn all that!" Something in that smile of his stopped her. "Wait! You're teasing me, aren't you? They haven't twenty-four articles!"

"Of course, they don't." She scowled, ready to scold, but Gary continued. "As I said. They have *one* article and twenty-four *ways to use* it."

A creak and a new shaft of sunlight interrupted the teasing. "Want out?" a voice called.

"Herbie!"

Gary rushed to her and helped Lucinda to her feet. "Come on. We need to get out of here while we have the chance. If she sees us, she might just decide that shooting is an excellent solution to her woes."

"We need those boxes, Gary." She took a couple of steps on her ankle and decided that while sore and stiff, she could walk. The packet of letters lay nearby, and she snatched them up as well.

"It's just stuff. I'll replace it."

Ignoring him, she reached for the suitcase handle. "It's potential *evidence*. Just like one of those detective stories. The police will need to see what was in my room."

"They probably already saw it." Gary tried to take the suitcase, but Lucinda refused to budge. "Get the boxes, Gary. We can hide them on the other side of Mrs. Wilson's house if we have to, but get them out of here before Ruby—"

"Ruby ain't here," Herbie broke in. "She took off in a hurry. When you guys didn't come out, I tried the door. It's locked. So, I went lookin' 'round for an open window and heard you'ns in here."

With that news, Gary hefted the box of books and carried it over to the double doors that now filled the cellar with natural light. "Time to go."

"Where?"

He looked down-right frightening as his jaw grew rigid and he ground out through clenched teeth, "The police."

EIGHTEEN

When Gary lifted the last box of books off the ground and turned around, he nearly dropped them again. There, Cinda stood frozen in place, eyes wide, staring at something just out of sight. As he took a step closer, he saw them. Ruby and Mrs. Smith.

"Ruby, I'm going to need your father's gun again."

"You can't shoot them out here, Mother," Ruby hissed. "The neighbors will see."

With a reproving look on her face, the woman turned to her daughter. "Get the gun out of your pocketbook right now, young lady." Listening to her, one would assume a small child had taken a candy without permission.

To his dismay, Ruby fumbled with the clasp. Dismay increased as he saw Herbie creeping up behind the women—with a bucket in hand! Just as Ruby reached a trembling hand into the pocketbook, water from the bucket hit her from behind.

Both women screamed. Mrs. Smith dove for the gun as it fell to the ground. Gary and Cinda dove for it as well. Cinda cried, "I'll stop her! Get the gun!"

As he dragged the thing away from Ruby's outstretched hand, Gary said, "No. I think I'll take control of that."

"Give me my father's gun!"

Muffled from the grass, a hard, cold voice growled, "You little fool. You've ruined everything."

"But Mother, he has *Father's gun*!" Indignation transformed into a whine. "He's pointing it at me!" Instead of showing fear, the girl stamped her foot and planted her hands on her hips. "You give me back my father's gun right now, Garrison Prince!"

Another voice broke into the melee. "Mother! What on earth? Lucinda Ashton, get off my poor mother!"

"Opal, dear, go into the house, up to your room, and close the windows."

"But—"

"Do as Mother says, for pity's sake!" Ruby lunged at Gary, but he held the gun pointed upward and out of reach. The girl actually jumped for it—repeatedly. "Or are you tall enough to get that gun?"

"No, Ruby! Opal is going *inside* this minute." The moment they heard the screen door close, Mrs. Smith turned her head so she could be heard better. "Opal has nothing to do with this. Do you understand me?"

Oddly enough, Gary realized he did. In that moment, he knew exactly what had happened. "Opal didn't go into the back of the theater, did she? She came later and in through the side door while all eyes were on the cast arrivals."

Cinda froze. "Then Ruby did get past Joe? Sun blindness?"

"No. Mrs. Smith has hair much like yours. I imagine hers was as light as Opal's when she was younger. *She* came into the theater dressed in your uniform. *She* shot Eva and Helen and Detective Lindstrom." He turned to Ruby. "Who killed Joe?"

"No one! I just hit him on the head when he was trying to grab Opal."

"Be quiet, Ruby."

But Ruby wouldn't be quiet. "He wasn't supposed to *die*. I had to do something, so I grabbed one of the shoes in my hand—one of *Cinder's* shoes—and whacked him hard across the temple. It worked! He just stood there for a moment, put a hand to his head, stumbled forward, and sat down hard."

"But why did you have Cinda's shoes? Why did you have them *then* if your mother wore a uniform that you changed into and out of again?"

"Don't, Ruby."

Ruby ignored her mother and spat out an answer. "Because I had to get the uniform out of there. I was going to give it to Mother and hurry on out again, but Opal came in, and that man was following her! I had to hit him, but he was *alive*! I did not kill *anyone!*"

Mrs. Smith tried to roll over, but Herbie plunked down on her heels. "Stay put."

Another woman came out from the house next door. "I don't know what's going on over here, but I've sent my boy for the police. Won't have these kinds of shenanigans going on around here. This is a respect—Miss Ashton?" The woman stepped closer. "Why are you sitting on Mrs. Smith?"

"She tried to threaten us with the gun Gary is holding," Lucinda said as if stating that they were playing a game of tag or hide-and-seek.

"Well, I never!" A look at Gary prompted a gasp. "But you're—you're—!"

"Gary Prinz, ma'am. Sorry for the disturbance, and we appreciate you calling for the police."

"My friend, Mildred Holmes, has a telephone. He's calling from—oh, look. There's the car now."

He didn't have much time. Turning back to Ruby, Gary demanded, "But why kill Eva? Was she aiming for me? For Cinda?"

"Oh, no!" A high-pitched giggle that reeked of lunacy

filled the air. "Mother's a crack-shot. She got who she wanted. First, Eva, then Helen. With them out of the way, we'll be called to fill a couple of lesser roles. Then later, if we don't get better parts—"

"Silence!"

Mrs. Smith needn't have shouted. With the police's arrival and the chaos that ensued, Gary couldn't hear the rest of Ruby's confession, anyway. Gary watched as Cinda led one officer aside and whispered something. The man looked up at the house, back at her, and over at where two other officers were leading the Smith women off to the police's Studebaker.

Should have realized that police departments use Studebakers, too.

A moment later, Cinda disappeared into the house. Gary moved closer to that officer and asked, "Is she going for Opal?"

"She says Opal Smith didn't know what her mother and sister did. We have to talk to her, but then we'll probably let her go if both the mother and sister agree."

"I think they were telling the truth. They seem to protect her for reasons I don't understand." Gary looked back at both the women, now squabbling as the officers ordered them into the car. "I don't think either of those women are… quite right."

"That's for a judge to decide. I heard the girl say something about fooling us into thinking it was Miss Ashton, so I think the D.A. made a good call dropping the case against her."

"There *wasn't* anything but circumstantial evidence that made no sense."

"Dunno. Wasn't in on that. Just know it isn't easy to know why the detectives do what they do, but they don't make many mistakes like that. Something pointed to her, if you don't mind my saying so."

Despite his desire to argue and protest, Gary realized it wouldn't do any good. Instead, he sent Herbie to the car with the boxes and went inside to help Cinda with Opal. The girl positively refused to leave her room until Gary assured her that her mother was on the way to talk to the police and wanted Opal to cooperate. "They don't suspect you of anything, of course, but it's important that they ask a few questions anyway."

Slow, heartbreaking tears spilled from the girl's eyes. "Will they call my father? Ask him to come? *Please*?" She leaned forward and said in a horrible whisper. "I've heard Mother and Ruby talking. I think Mother might have..." The tears turned to sobs. "Oh, why did we ever come to this terrible place!"

Not such a Dumb Dora after all...

By the time Lucinda had finally climbed the stairs to "her" bedroom at the Cohens' house, her brain had become mush. She stood at the window, watching Gary's car drive down the hill and away from her. He and Herbie would come again tomorrow afternoon and they'd make plans and calls—official ones—for a small wedding. *Her* wedding.

It might be a bit early for bed, but exhaustion pulled her away from the window and almost unaware of her actions, she undressed, climbed beneath the covers, and relaxed for the first time that day. *Tomorrow I won't have a hearing, a proposal, a house viewing, and a showdown in front of my old boarding house. Tomorrow I can relax...* The rest of that thought never materialized.

She dreamed of a leisurely morning. A long, hot bath, followed by a filling breakfast, and a little time in the sun on the terrace before lunch. Later that afternoon, she and Gary would begin that planning.

Mrs. Cohen had other ideas.

The moment she'd stepped out of her room, the woman

had begun a whirlwind day. After a *quick* bath and a breakfast that she almost didn't taste, their driver had whisked them away to a small, well-lit studio where a snooty woman, a very strange man, and a few obsequious girls spent three hours draping and pinning diaphanous layers of fabric over silken cloth draped over her half-clothed body.

Mrs. Cohen held up sketch after sketch as the man stared, drew, and stared some more before ripping off the final idea and flinging it at her. Each time, Lucinda found something to say she liked. "That neckline is lovely" or "I particularly love the longer length of that skirt. The petal treatment of the hem is also sweet."

That word, "sweet," had nearly gotten them kicked out. When a length of embroidered chiffon—a good twelve feet, at least—was brought in, Lucinda gasped. "Oh, that is exquisite!"

"Finally!" the man crowed. "We have something the lady approves of. Put that on her!"

And the torture commenced. After that, as long as what he came up with wasn't hideous, Lucinda vowed within herself to praise it to the skies, truthful or not. Duplicity, however, proved unnecessary. *And a good thing, too, after I scolded Gary about it.*

The final sketch showed the square neckline she'd admitted to admiring with detail mimicking the petal tipped skirt hemline and complimentary sleeves that mostly allowed for bare arms. The bridal cap holding an enormous veil also alluded to the same design pattern. With just the right shoes, she'd feel like the princess Hollywood would still try to make her out to be.

"I've never seen anything so beautiful in my life."

After all the huffs, snorts, sighs, and wails, the man turned on her and beamed. "I will—the moment you put it on for the final fitting—I will have seen something even more beautiful than the dress. You in it."

Had each word not rung with sincerity, Lucinda would have laughed. The three obsequious assistants all stood, gaping at him. Even Madame Snoot shot a look of surprise before turning up her nose and informing Mrs. Cohen that the dress wouldn't be ready for three weeks, and even then, only if Lucinda came for each fitting on the day required. "Each day she is late, is another week. We maintain a tight schedule."

"She'll be here."

The statement made Lucinda feel as if she were twelve again and had gotten caught throwing eggs at Mrs. Dexter's mean old bull. Again. They hadn't made her scrub the bull, but she had been required to clean and scrub the chicken coop—inside and out—the very next Saturday. She'd never been fond of chickens since.

Her stomach clenched and her breathing… Well, was she? A great gulp of air hinted maybe she hadn't been. Mrs. Cohen gave her a funny look when someone squeaked out, "Gary won't expect me to keep *chickens*, will he?"

That someone must have been her.

"I doubt it, Cinda… come on. Let's get you home." The woman may have commented to the others about a stressful week. Lucinda couldn't be sure. All she could think of were rows of beady eyes lined up along a chicken fence, beaks punctuating the spaces between those eyes, and the certainty that every last one of the creatures waited to pounce on the slaughterer of their sisters' unhatched chicks.

She shuddered and burst into tears.

Gary paced the Cohens' terrace. Albert had gone to work that morning, as any responsible studio owner might. The ladies had gone shopping and returned with Cinda in what for her amounted to hysterics. "It's all hitting at once," Miriam said as she led Cinda upstairs. "She'll feel better after a nap, I imagine." And so, he paced.

Jervis brought out coffee, a sandwich, and the evening papers that ruffled in the breeze. "They'll be dining late, sir. I thought you might like something while you wait."

A glance at his watch showed just after five. "Thank you." He pulled the first paper near him. *The Los Angeles Examiner.* Instead of a headline announcing the capture of the Taj Mahal Murderer, it announced, AIMEE M'PHERSON BELIEVED DROWNED. Gary's gut clenched as he read about the last sighting of the popular Angelus Temple's charismatic woman preacher.

Below the fold came the lesser headline. STARLETS' MOTHER KILLS IN INSANE RAGE. The breeze grew stiffer, forcing Gary to fight to keep the pages flat as he read.

Friday night's murderous shooting spree has dark motives. According to sources within the Los Angeles police department and neighbors of the accused, police believe Ada Smith (Mrs.) shot and killed actress Eva Labelle (Edith Flint) and starlet Helen Fenwick in a ploy to give her own daughters Opal Sterling (Smith) and Ruby Sterling (Smith) an advantage at upcoming roles in Imperial Studios' next picture.

According to sources, Mrs. Smith is known back in New York state as an excellent shot. Rather than a wonder that she was able to fire and kill two people at such a distance, it seems that the true mystery is how she missed killing Detective Carl Lindstrom of the Los Angeles Police Department.

The fourth victim of the Taj Mahal Massacre—

Gary huffed at that. While three people had been killed, it hadn't been indiscriminate. "Sensationalist reporting."

However, he continued reading despite his disgust.

The fourth victim of the Taj Mahal Massacre, Joseph

Gorsky, appears to have died from smoke inhalation. Rumors among theater employees hint at his having been hit over the head and stunned. At the same time, the electricity was cut, resulting in the fire that destroyed most of the building. While many employees first thought the fire was the work of one former and disgruntled employee, Theodore Wolski, witnesses to Miss Ruby Sterling (Smith)'s free and public confession state that she "didn't mean to hurt him, only stop him from accosting my sister." If the young woman's statements can be believed, his "accosting" would have taken the form of preventing the woman from cutting the wire and escaping with the gun used in the evening's killing spree.

"Again, awful, but not much of a spree… And I think they are mixing the ladies."

Miriam's voice startled him as she stepped onto the terrace. "A bit sensational, isn't it?"

"You've read it?"

"Jervis brought me a copy that I read before coming down."

A quick scan told of a Mr. William Smith leaving New York to retrieve his eldest daughter and return home with her. It was supposed that both women would be sent to a mental institution should they be found guilty.

With that information in mind, Gary refolded the paper and set it aside with his empty plate atop it. *When did I eat that sandwich?*

"Lucinda is fine. She fell asleep after mumbling something about being ridiculous. However…" Miriam smiled at Gary. "I do believe she has a powerful fear of chickens, and I wouldn't ever suggest she consider even looking at a live one."

"Chickens?"

Miriam reached for a cup of coffee that Jervis brought her and nodded as the man carried away the newspapers and empty plate. "Something about being literally henpecked at age twelve."

Disappointment raised up, stretched, and settled somewhere in his middle. "I'd half-expected to have a few—for eggs and maybe a few fryers for Sunday dinners. I imagined Sundays in our little church, a nice short sermon, and a walk or leisurely drive home to a slow-roasted chicken. A touch of country living but still in a nice town, you know?"

"If you want chickens, you'd better be prepared to clean coops, gather eggs, feed, and butcher the things yourself. If you're not, I wouldn't be surprised if Lucinda handed you back that ring."

"Why would I give Gary back my ring?" Lucinda breezed in no longer looking wrung out and hung to dry. As if the most natural thing in the world, she paused by Gary's chair and kissed his cheek before settling in. "I quite like it—and what it signifies."

"Miriam informs me that you don't share my dream of chicken farming."

"That isn't a dream, Gary. It's a nightmare." She scowled at him before beaming up at Jervis who arrived with a glass of milk and two gingersnap cookies on a plate. "Thank you, Jervis." She eyed the man. "You would never expect your wife to suffer at the tyranny of chickens, would you?"

"Of course, not, miss. Most ungallant."

Cinda turned to him with a smug smile. "Will you rise to that challenge, Gary? Would you suffer the charge of ungallant?"

"Never. If chickens reside on Chester Avenue, then they will be my sole responsibility." He reached for her hand. "Speaking of responsibility, when do you plan to allow me to assume the responsibility of being your devoted husband?"

He'd expected her to insist on some ridiculously long engagement—six months or a year or more. Instead, Cinda turned to Miriam and asked, "Did that man say the dress would be done in four or six weeks?"

"Three, although, I imagine I could impress on him the urgency of sooner if necessary."

His fiancée turned to him, all smiles and confidence again. "How does the third Saturday in June sound—whatever date that is?"

He turned to Miriam. "Would you consider looking after Herbie for a few days near the end of June?"

"We'd be glad to. Albert's taken a liking to the boy. I suspect he'll want to hire Herbie over the summer—errand boy and such."

Gary stared at the date on the paper. May 18th, 1926. Quick calculations gave him a date. "June nineteenth, then."

Lucinda nodded and gave him a smile that might as well have been a kiss. "June nineteenth."

NINETEEN

They'd managed to secure a small church in Pasadena for the ceremony, Cinda's former church not being eager to have the press attention, and the wait had only been semi-torturous. After all, with her getting married in just four weeks, Cinda hadn't needed to find another job. Gary's classes weren't to start until September, and that meant two entire months of learning to be a family after the wedding and a month of just being together beforehand.

Now, with light streaming through windows and a room half-full of friends to celebrate with them, Gary waited, knees quaking, as every eye in the room watched him. *I could never have been a theater actor. All those eyes…* He felt himself go green as he realized that one day he'd stand before a congregation to share the Scriptures with them.

Herbie and Albert stood beside him, waiting for Patty Anderson and Cinda to come in through the doors. An organ played "Love Divine, All Loves Excelling," and it set Gary's teeth on edge. *If Jesus' love is divine, then why are we playing that hymn when I'm about to marry my earthly love. It seems irreverent.* A prick in his conscience told him all. *A reminder, Lord? Is that it? I'm not to allow my love for Cinda to supersede my devotion to You?*

Patty entered the room in a pale-yellow frock that reminded Gary of lemonade. A glance at Herbie nearly made him laugh aloud. If the boy had been smitten at the small engagement party the Cohens had thrown them, this would be his undoing. As if to torment the boy further, Patty winked at Herbie as she moved aside to make room for Cinda's entrance.

Undone? Completely. There was no other word for it. Gary stood, transfixed as Cinda stepped into the room in a dress so lovely he finally understood where people got the ridiculous notion that angels were feminine—beautiful. Angelic was the only word for her. A veil trailed out behind several feet, and all his heretofore opinions regarding the wastefulness of lengthy veils faded into mist and vanished.

Does every man think there couldn't be a more beautiful bride in the world than his?

Hours passed, or was it only minutes, before she reached his side and Patty began fussing with the veil. At least the voluminous skirts of his mother's era were gone. Cinda's didn't even reach her ankles. *Mother would have said she has a well-turned ankle.*

In contrast to his nervousness, Cinda exuded serenity. She gazed first at him and then the minister before turning back to him, that kissable smile never leaving her lips. *If you're not careful, soon-to-be Mrs. Prinz, I'll kiss you before the minister gives me permission. Right here. Right in front of everyone.*

The smile transformed into a smirk.

Oh, how I love you, Cinda Ashton.

"Repeat after me. I, Gary…"

"—INTRODUCE to you Mr. and Mrs. Gary Prinz."

For a month, Lucinda had imagined that someday she would carry a baby, and like Mary, she'd treasure each moment of pregnancy, birth, and motherhood in her heart. Yet, here she was, dashing down the aisle beside Gary, already treasuring the moment Mrs. Cohen pinned on her bridal cap, adjusted her veil, and told her how beautiful she looked. She'd already found a perfect little place in her heart where she'd store the memory of Gary's expression when he first saw her enter the chapel. Right beside it, the memory of his strong, sure voice cracking as he said, "I do" would live forever.

Just outside the front doors, Gary pulled her out of sight and kissed her until her hair Marceled itself beneath her bridal cap. "I love you, Mrs. Prinz."

As a child in Oregon, friends' parents had sometimes called each other mister or missus. It had seemed so silly back then. Now, Lucinda already wanted him to say it again. "And I love you, Mr. Prinz."

Herbie found them first, his face beaming up at them. "Now we're really a family."

Hugging him, Cinda whispered, "I'm so happy you're going to be a part of it. The perfect wedding gift."

"Never thought I'd be someone's weddin' present, but all right. If you say so."

Guests swarmed the front steps, congratulating them, smiling as a photographer took a photograph and scowling as another from one of the papers stole one at the same time. There'd be no reception—not a real one. She and Gary had decided against it, despite the Cohens insisting on arranging one for them. "You bought my dress—and an expensive thing it was, too. That was enough," she'd insisted.

Instead, just as soon as they'd seen off their guests, the Prinzes, a Grant—for now, anyway—and the Cohens drove to the house on Chester Avenue and strolled up the walk, chattering. "I never knew getting married could be so exhausting! I feel like I've been in the theater for three films straight!"

Gary squeezed her hand as he led her up the steps and

said, "I, for one, am glad you won't ever have to sell cigarettes and candy again."

Once inside, Mrs. Cohen bustled Lucinda off to the bedroom where they removed the cap and veil and tried to smooth her hair. "This whole day feels like a fairy tale, doesn't it?"

A mouth full of hairpins made it impossible for Mrs. Cohen to speak, but she gave Lucinda a look that said, "What do you mean?"

"This dress, the church, the flowers—don't pretend you didn't order them. I know Gary didn't, and I certainly didn't."

The woman's eyes said, "A bride needs flowers" even if Lucinda couldn't understand Mrs. Cohen's mumbles around the pins.

"And then Gary… such a handsome and kind man." She giggled. "A real *Prinz* of a fellow."

For a moment, Mrs. Cohen sounded like she'd choked on a hairpin.

"And you're like my own fairy godmother."

Mrs. Cohen pulled the last two pins from her mouth and said, "Perhaps fairly godmotherly, but…"

Herbie knocked and poked his head in the door. "Are ya comin'? He's pacin'."

She turned to face him—the boy who already felt like a son. Would Gary's lawyer really be able to arrange for a legal adoption? Mr. Hollister seemed to think so, but what if he couldn't? The freckle-faced lad just beamed at her. "You'd think he hadn't already gotcha or sumpin'!"

Your speech becomes atrocious when you're excited.

Still, Herbie had a point. When Lucinda moved into the dining room, flowers filled the room—or so it seemed. She shot an accusatory look at Mrs. Cohen, but the woman refused to look ashamed.

"If I can't have the fun of creating a reception, I can at least order a few flowers."

A bower is more like it.

"It's lovely, Miriam." Gary slipped an arm around her, and Lucinda both blushed and melted into him. "Thank you."

He offered a prayer—one that seemed to make the Cohens uncomfortable and Herbie beam. "Just think," the boy blurted out on the heels of the amen. "A month ago, I was livin' on the streets and Cindy was in jail. Now, we're all sittin' in a flower shop eatin' cake." He eyed the center of the table with exaggerated interest. "Or we should be."

"I'll take that hint," Lucinda said as she picked up a plate and a cake server. "Who would like a slice?"

Gary held her chair for her once she'd passed each person a small plate of cake. Mrs. Cohen brought out chicken salad sandwiches and a fruit salad, made by her cook. Instinct said to insist Herbie eat his lunch before tackling the cake, but she couldn't make herself do it. She needn't have worried, though. The moment he'd swiped the last crumb from the little plate, he tucked into his sandwich and salad with gusto.

"Herbie does make a point." Gary stared at the sandwich in his hand as if it revealed secrets only to him. He looked up and met her gaze. "We've a lot to be thankful for—and a lot to pray for. I spoke with Mr. Smith this week. He said he knew his wife could become unreasonably obsessive about things—such as insisting on moving to Hollywood so the girls could be in pictures—but he'd never imagined her going so far as to kill to get what she wanted. He's given a deposition, and as both his wife and Ruby have stated that Opal knew nothing about the events behind the theater debacle, the judge is allowing him to take her back to New York."

Relief washed through her. "Opal never was as nasty as Ruby. She always seemed a little more apologetic when she tried to insist I do something that, as a boarder, I was not obligated to do. Now I think she was put up to it by her stronger-willed sister."

Silence descended over the table. Just as Lucinda would

have commented on the warmth of the day, Gary leaned back in his chair and said, "This situation had many lessons for me, but the most disheartening was that I am not suited to be the next Hercule Poirot or Sherlock Holmes. Some things I still don't understand." He winked at Lucinda. "We could have been Tommy and Tuppence."

"Who?" Lucinda speared a cube of melon. "I recognize the other two, but…"

"Tommy and Tuppence are a team who become amateur sleuths who are hired to find someone. They will eventually marry." Gary winked. "We beat them to it! But they found their missing woman. I just missed every clue there was. In hindsight, Ruby should have been my primary suspect."

An argument erupted. Mr. Cohen insisted they had considered her a possibility, but she had not been in back when the first shots were fired. "There was no reason to imagine Mrs. Smith would come to the theater and shoot anyone."

"Although she did lock me in the cellar that day, and Ruby had my uniform. I should have assumed there could be some connection," Lucinda put in. "And who knew she could fit into my clothes!" A thought explained it all to her. "Oh! My too-big skirts so I could have extra length. She probably unpicked the stitching."

"I still don't understand why she'd wear your shoes," Mrs. Cohen argued. "Why take those?"

"She doesn't have the required black ones, and someone would notice. Mr. Goldman is particular on that point. I've only seen her wear brown for daily wear and tan for church. I suppose she gave Ruby the uniform to take back and that's why Ruby was holding my shoes when she hit poor Joe."

Again, Mrs. Cohen argued. "But they seem to have thought out the scheme in surprising detail when locking you in didn't work."

There, Gary spoke up. "I think they had this planned all

along, and Ruby thought up a way to make it easier—get you to let them in instead of all the costume changes."

"I'd become convinced Walter Walker was involved somehow. He acted so guilty that day at Traumwood," Mr. Cohen said. "I wonder what that was about."

"He has mob ties," Gary said. "I suspect he was concerned about the threats he made. Guilt does that."

"He *should* feel guilty for threatening to kill you!" Lucinda's expostulation prompted smiles by all but Herbie who nodded his agreement. "And if he doesn't want people to look into his affairs, he ought to think of that before making threats."

Mrs. Cohen bemoaned how long it took her to understand Lucinda's cryptic comments. There, Gary jumped in again. "Ah, yes. But you actually figured them out. And Cinda was clever enough to try to hint about them. I missed them both."

Gary sounded a little more despondent about his lack of detective prowess than Lucinda liked to hear, so she laid a hand on his arm and said, "But you will be learning to discover the mysteries of Scripture and make them plain to the rest of us. Isn't that far superior?"

Mrs. Cohen looked at her husband. Albert shot a glance at Lucinda, who trained her eyes on Herbie. The boy swept the room with one confused glance and threw up his hands. "I gots nothin', folks."

While the others laughed and began making plans for how they'd spend the next week, Gary leaned over, kissed Lucinda's cheek, and said, "I'll be learning the mysteries of being a husband to the sweetest wife alive, too. *That* is far superior to the wonders of who stole your shoe and left it in the alley."

The End

HISTORICAL NOTES & ACKNOWLEDGEMENTS

Los Angeles was a paradox in the 1920s. Just as Hollywood became the center of the movie scene, it also became a center of spiritual awakening and revival. The Bible Institute of Los Angeles (now known as BIOLA) began under the oversight of the Church of the Open Door, and as I wrote the story, I couldn't find out who was the pastor of the church that year. I reached out to the church, and their archivist, Judy Cocoris, informed me that this was because they had no pastor between the time R. A. Torrey resigned in 1924 and December of 1926 when Reverend John McNeill became pastor. I'm so grateful to her for such quick assistance.

Aimee Semple McPherson's disappearance preceded Agatha Christie's famous eleven-day disappearance by over six months. Ms. McPherson was the minister at Angelus Temple and the founder of the Foursquare Church. I did extensive research on her disappearance, and despite the rumors of the time, I did not find evidence against her to be compelling enough to prove her guilty of faking the kidnapping—certainly not the evidence the police and legal teams tried to use.

However, as I read the story, it seemed plausible that either she or Agatha Christie could have gotten the idea from the other. When I discovered that Dame Agatha's disappearance *followed* McPherson's, I couldn't help but wonder if she had tried to test how likely it was to disappear like that. It flies in the face of the prevailing theory of depression and a "fugue state," but the idea *almost* made me change the entire plot of this book. Still, one wonders...

I kept as many of the locations and details of 1926 Los Angeles, Hollywood, Santa Monica, and Pasadena as accurate to the time as I could. Los Angeles first planted the jacaranda trees in the 20s and 30's, so I had to include my favorite part of visiting the Los Angeles basin—those lovely purple-flowered trees. I didn't want to use Grauman's Chinese Theater for the scene of the crime because of the negative aspects of such a crime *and* because it was still being built in 1926. I needed this book to take place before Warner Brothers released *The Jazz Singer* and "talkies" became the Hollywood rage. I alluded to coming changes but did not specify exactly what they were. "Talking pictures" were what I meant.

The Santa Monica pier did have an enormous roller-coaster at the time, The Whirlwind Dipper, which replaced The Blue Streak from a few years before. The carousel was also a prominent part of the "Pleasure Pier," but alas, Cinda didn't get to ride then. Perhaps they took Herbie before he and Gary began their fall studies!

Pasadena had become home for many wealthy members of Los Angeles society—those who wanted a more respectable and sedate life than they could find in Beverly Hills. I originally put the home Gary and Lucinda bought on Orange Grove Boulevard, but because it has become known as "Millionaires' Row," I shifted the choice to one on Chester Avenue instead. In fact, I even chose specific houses that are for sale today just to ensure they were there.

Finding all the details—the gun that someone might have brought home from WWI, the dress lengths and styles, *stockings*, and the salaries of Hollywood stars of the time took hours. I've no doubt that I both made small errors (I hope small!) and took a few too many licenses (there is no park near where Cinda would have lived—and likely no boarding house there at the time, either), but I strove to stick to as much accuracy as humanly possible. Named churches and restaurants are real. I almost used an actual fire captain's name but didn't. Imperial and Sunset Studios (by their exact names as written) have never existed as far as my research informs me. Pickfair (named for Mary Pickford and Douglas Fairbanks) did. And the annexation issue that Gary mentioned—it was a thing many Beverly Hills stars fought against and won by a vote of (reportedly) 507 to 337.

Of everything I learned during research, the paradox between the speakeasies and revivals of the time surprised me most. I hope I did history justice.

ABOUT THE AUTHOR

Chautona Havig lives in an oxymoron, escapes into imaginary worlds that look startlingly similar to ours and writes the stories that emerge. An irrepressible optimist, Chautona sees everything through a kaleidoscope of It's a Wonderful Life sprinkled with fairy tales. Find her on the web and say howdy—if you can remember how to spell her name.

facebook.com/chautonahavig
instagram.com/ChautonaHavig
amazon.com/author/chautonahavig
bookbub.com/authors/chautona-havig
goodreads.com/Chautona
pinterest.com/chautonahavig

ALSO BY CHAUTONA HAVIG

The Independence Islands Series

Christmas on Breakers Point (series prequel)

Dual Power of Convenience (Merriweather Island)

Bookers on the Rocks (Elnora Island)

Flipping Hearts (Hopper Island)

Finding a Memory (Sparrow Island) — Coming 2022

Meddlin' Madeline Mysteries (5 Book Series)

The Hartfield Mysteries (4 Book Series)

Ever After Mysteries

The Last Gasp

The Nutcracker's Suite

The Ransom of Grete — Coming 2022

BOOKS IN THE EVER AFTER MYSTERIES SERIES

The Last Gasp by Chautona Havig

A Giant Murder by Marji Laine

When the Pilot Falls by April Hayman

Murder at the Empire by Cathe Swanson

The Lost Dutchman's Secret by Rebekah Jones

The Nutcracker's Suite by Chautona Havig

Silencing the Siren by Denise L. Barela

Slashed Canvas by Liz Tolsma

A GIANT MURDER

A SNEAK PEEK AT THE NEXT EVER AFTER MYSTERY!

MARJI LAINE

ONE

D*allas, Texas, 1926*

Always be prepared for anything.

Josephine Jacobs could almost hear her mom's reminder. But how could she have prepared for fisticuffs in the middle of an elegant event? She crouched next to her serving station in the modern chrome kitchen as yet another crash of pans made her flinch.

The guests of the elegant affair on the other side of the swinging door must be hearing all of this. Maybe the band in the Century Ballroom drowned it out. Josie poked her head above the counter.

"Haven't you seen the paper, Goose? I'm a giant in my field." TG Taggert, the host of the gala, grabbed the smaller man by his white chef's collar and shoved him against a shelf full of cookware. He pushed off the unit and shoved a fist toward Mr. Taggert. "You're not going to get away with this."

Mr. Taggert reached to the side and then backhanded the man across the face.

Josie ducked at the violence.

"You don't have any say, my friend." Taggert's voice had an ugly sound. Another crash followed Mr. Taggert's shout.

Josie peeked out again. How could she not? If nothing else, she wanted to make sure the fight wasn't moving closer to her.

The chef's nose showed blood. "I'm not your friend. And they aren't your beans."

Beans? She hadn't been paying attention when the fight broke out, but really. Beans?

Mr. Taggert gathered the chef's collar in a meaty fist again. "They are my goose-laid, golden eggs, Ganderson. What do you think you'll do about it?"

The chef's face looked positively blistered, but he didn't explode. "I'll kill you before I let you take my recipes and sell them in your horrible cans."

Mr. Taggert threw his head back and laughed. Almost a pleasant sound. He patted the chef on the cheek he'd just hit as though the man were a good dog.

"Face it, Goose, you made a gamble. You went up against the big guys and you lost. Fair and square." Then he turned his back on the man.

Josie ducked again behind the counter until Mr. Taggert swaggered back into the ballroom. She rose, noticing for the first time that she hadn't been the only worker hiding behind the counters. Both dishwashers appeared from behind the drying racks and three other women, two cooks, and an assistant squatted behind the little cutting island.

"We'll see about that," Anton growled as he looked around at all of them. His nose still dripped, and it did nothing to smooth his temper. "Get back to work."

Now that shout had definitely been heard in the ballroom, but Josie wasn't interested in waiting to see what happened next. She grabbed a platter of bite-sized sandwiches and scurried out to begin serving.

For the next hour, Josie wandered from tier to tier in the three-level room. Groups of men and women talked, danced, or watched the others. She mingled admiring furs, elegant gowns, and jewelry that she'd only heard stories about.

"Those smoked salmon rolls are positively soggy." Mr. Taggert himself stood over Josie.

Her spine iced down to her ankles. "I'm sorry, sir."

The man's face softened. "What's your name, kid?"

She hadn't expected that. Was he going to complain about her? "Josephine Jacobs, sir."

He put his hand lightly on her shoulder. "You're not at fault, Josephine. Take them back to the kitchen and collect something else. I'll speak to Anton myself."

She heaved out her relief and obeyed.

Chef Anton caught her abrupt return and glared as she set aside the full tray, but he didn't say anything. With a full tray of deviled eggs, she reentered the Century Ballroom. At least, she didn't have to worry about these being soggy.

Josie moved to the middle level with her tray. Her friend and coworker, Penelope gave her a wink from the lower level. She'd squealed when their boss from the restaurant downstairs had asked them to serve up here tonight. And no wonder she was excited. With her honey-blonde bob and her perky grin, Penelope fit in perfectly with the style of the society women, even without their long silk and satin gowns and shimmering jewels. And the gentlemen constantly surrounded her.

Josie was a flat tire compared to cutie-pie Penelope, but they both owed a big thank you to their boss. Not that she disliked her kitchen job in the basement restaurant, but being asked to serve at this gala, even at the last minute, was something out of a dream.

She moved to a group of women wearing long-draped gowns. None of the flapper folderol that she'd heard about, but elegance to the extreme. Avoiding direct eye contact, per the kitchen manager's instructions, she took in the ornate chandeliers that hung from the painted ceiling.

Most of the guests didn't glance at her and certainly didn't speak with her, not even a thank you, but that was to be expected. She'd been reminded that she should blend into the carpet, and with the black dress that they'd given her to wear, she would have. That was, until the kitchen supervisor had tied a starched white apron around her waist and plopped a white cap with a lace edge on her head. She'd have rather stayed in black, completely unseen, and simply bear witness to this exciting event.

More people moved to the dance floor as the band played. A familiar voice began to sing, and Josie looked down to the stage. Harper Davis. Last Josie had heard, the girl had tried to go to Hollywood, but with big acts like Gene Austin singing from time to time here at the Adolphus Hotel, Harper was in good company.

She and Josie had been in school together from their primary years on up, but that was where the comparison between them ended. Harper had always been beautiful, strikingly so with her brilliant blue eyes, even with the mouse-colored waves she'd always worn long. Now as a blonde with a fashionable bob and wearing opera-length white gloves, a bright red dress, and matching lipstick in a perfect cupid's bow, she was made for the silver screen. If only the movies had the sound to also share her gorgeous voice.

Josie, on the other hand had always been too much. Too short. Too clumsy. Too plain. She still wore her long brunette hair in a braid down her back, curled into a tight bun for working purposes.

And she had a job to do. She forced herself to stop daydreaming and get back to serving. She approached a group of men with her tray, then hesitated when she realized Mr. Taggert was in the group. Did she want to encounter him again?

Some of the other men snagged eggs from her tray, so she had little choice. She held it out to the host. "I don't want any of that stuff." He waved it away, then plunked down his glass in the middle of the tray, moving several appetizers out of the way. He put his hand at her back and walked down the side stairs with her. "I don't like all these sweet, fizzy drinks, and I detest iced tea, but I have a special bottle of ginger ale that I prefer. It's in my suite. Can you fill this glass with crushed ice in the kitchen and go pour me a fresh drink?"

"Uh... I..."

"It's only on the floor below us, 1801. Won't take you more than five minutes. There's a key in the kitchen, and I'll clear it with Anton if he gets a bug in his britches about it."

Josie's face warmed slightly at his choice of words, but she would certainly honor the request of her benefactor for the evening. "Of course, Mr. Taggert."

She gave him a tight smile and made her way to the kitchen where she abandoned the tray of egg halves. After dumping the remains of his drink into the sink, she added the requested crushed ice and went in search of the key.

The woman who seemed to be second-in-command stood eye-to-eye with the chef and had silvery hair in a sweaty bob that curled around thick cheeks which matched her middle. She stirred a syrupy mixture at the corner stove.

"I'm looking for the key to Mr. Taggert's suite?"

The woman gave her a sidelong look without response.

Josie held up the glass. "He'd like another ginger ale."

The woman still didn't respond but tilted her head to her left. A ring of keys hung on a hook beside the pantry door.

Josie started to ask which key she should use, but the woman had moved to another counter where a cook was rolling chicken bites into triangles of puff pastry. She would have to figure this out alone.

www.ingramcontent.com/pod-product-compliance
Lightning Source LLC
LaVergne TN
LVHW041929090826
845145LV00017B/2300